GUNMEN

A Brittle and Ashe Adventure

GUNMEN

by Timothy Friend
A Brittle and Ashe Adventure

Published by BAM Books

BAM Books
Kansas City, MO
USA

www.bam-books.com

ISBN: 978-1-7359805-0-8 (print)
ISBN: 978-1-7359805-1-5 (ebook)

For Jenn-
My pardner to the end of the trail.

ONE

If it wasn't for a whore named Dottie, Charlie Brittle and I would never have taken up bounty hunting. At that time we owned and operated one of three saloons in the tiny town of Olvidados. The town didn't have people enough to keep one saloon in business, let alone three, and when you considered that ours was the least popular, it meant lean times for Charlie and me. I had won the place in a poker game in El Paso the year before and I'd been regretting it ever since.

Charlie and I were sitting in a couple of chairs under the porch awning out front of the saloon trying to stay cool when I heard Dottie step out behind us. She said, "I know that fella."

Charlie was leaning back in his chair with his feet up on the rail and his hat pulled low. He looked like he was napping, but I knew he was just figuring on our money troubles. Without raising his hat he said, "Dottie, what the hell are you doing here?"

"I'm drinking,w" Dottie said. "That's what you do in a saloon."

In addition to having three saloons, Olvidados had two dollar-a-poke whore houses. Dottie worked at one of them, but she didn't seem to care for whoring much and spent most of her time in our place. If anybody missed her they never came looking for her.

Charlie and she didn't get along. It wasn't that he had anything against whores, he just thought that since whoring was her occupation, she was lazy for not doing more of it. But she paid for her whiskey, and more often than not she was our only customer. So as much as she annoyed him he never ran her off.

I looked back at Dottie. She was about twenty, blonde, pretty going on plain. She tapped her finger against the wanted notice posted beside our front door.

We didn't have any law in Olvidados, so from time to time a deputy marshal would ride through to check on things. He'd been by a week ago and put up the paper. Generally they were supposed to be tacked up outside the Sheriff's office, or in pinch outside the bank or post office. Since we didn't have any of those I guess he figured a saloon was as good as any place.

The Notice read:

> **$1000 Reward to any person or persons who will deliver bank robber and murderer Arbo Cullins (Dead or Alive) to any sheriff of New Mexico.**
>
> **Cullins stands five foot ten inches, bearded with buck teeth and one milky eye.**

By now Charlie had turned around to look at the notice.

He scratched at his cheek, thinking. "How do you know him?"

Dottie put her hands on her hips and looked at him like he was stupid. "How you think? I fucked him. He come through about two weeks ago."

"You sure it was him?" I asked. "Not like there's a picture."

"I'm sure," Dottie said. "Had that milky eye just like it says. And he was so buck-toothed he could eat watermelon through a key-hole. Plus he said his name was Arbo."

"That does seem to clinch it," Charlie said. I didn't like the way Charlie was pondering this information.

"What are you thinking?" I asked.

"I'm thinking we could use a thousand dollars."

I wasn't hot on the idea of hunting down a killer. I'd had enough of getting shot at during my time as a shotgun messenger for Wells Fargo. Charlie used to scout for the army and quit, so I thought he felt the same. Lately though, I'd begun to wonder. He seemed to be getting restless the more we hung around Olvidados with nothing to do. I think he had imagined keeping the peace in a saloon would be a wild and wooly time. That not being the case, least not in our saloon, he was getting restless.

"Awful hard to pick up his trail after two weeks," I said, trying my best to be discouraging. Charlie nodded, and I was hopeful that might be the end of it.

Dottie said, "He told me he was going to work for his brother. Said he was the foreman out at the mine."

"Well, ain't you just a Goddamn fountain of information," I said.

"There's no call to take that tone with me, Owen Ashe. I'm just telling you what I know."

"Can't hurt to talk about," Charlie said.

"Talking ain't what I'm worried about," I said.

We went inside where it was cooler, but more depressing. Business was dead, as usual. When I'd acquired the place I pictured a polished bar with a big mirror behind it, maybe a few upstairs rooms where the public girls would entertain. What I got was a one room, raw-plank building that only counted as a saloon because the previous owner had laid a board across two barrels and put up a shelf of whiskey behind it.

The back corner was blocked off by a couple of hanging sheets where Charlie and I bunked. It was one step from sleeping in the alley, and I wasn't sure the alley wouldn't have been more comfortable.

Charlie went behind the bar and got a couple glasses. He had to stretch to reach the bottles on the shelf. Watching him do that was something that always amused me. It was about the only time I noticed his actual size. Charlie only stood about five foot eight in his boots, but always seemed bigger. He had a way of taking up a lot of space. Charlie poured two fingers of whiskey in each of our glasses, then came and sat down at the table. Dottie had followed us inside, listening as

Charlie tried to get me all the way over on the idea of manhunting. She sat down at the table like she had a stake in the matter.

"I don't think we're cut out to run no saloon," Charlie said.

Looking around at the place, it wasn't something I could argue. Everything had accumulated a blanket of dust from disuse. We only had three mismatched tables in the place. The chairs were turned up on the other two, and lately we had taken to leaving them there. It just seemed like wasted effort to take them down every morning, only to put them back every night never having been dusted by an ass.

"I'm not sure we're cut out to hunt men either," I said.

"Hell, I did it for the army," Charlie said.

"I thought that was why you quit," I said.

"I quit because the army was quick to kill Apache just for being Apache. That didn't seem like much of a reason to me. This Arbo fella is a murderer and thief. Throw in the reward, and I believe I can get behind a killing like that."

"Awful quick to decide on killing him. Shouldn't we at least try to capture him?"

Charlie grinned. "Hell, Owen. We can always try."

"But you don't figure he'll surrender."

"Would you? I believe I'd rather take a bullet than swing into nowhere on the end of a rope."

Dottie noisily supped the last of the whiskey from

her glass. "I sure wouldn't want to hang. Sounds just awful."

Dottie held her empty glass out to Charlie. He just looked at her. Dottie sighed, got up and went behind the bar.

"Suppose we go after him," I said. "What do we do with this place? We just close it up while we're gone? It don't make much, but it's better than nothing."

"It's exactly nothing," Charlie said. "Close it up. Put a match to it. I don't care. We ain't businessmen and we shouldn't have tried to be."

"I can watch the place," Dottie said.

Charlie let out an ugly laugh. "What the hell do you know about being a bartender?"

"It ain't that complicated," Dottie said. She glared at him as she tipped the bottle up and filled her glass. She sat the bottle down, then slapped the cork back in, picked up her glass with a flourish and arched an eyebrow at Charlie.

"Fine," Charlie said. "You can watch the place while we're gone."

"I guess we all get new jobs today," I said.

TWO

We rode side by side, headed for the copper mine just a few miles outside of Olvidados. The mine was the only reason the town existed. When it was producing at it's peak it had employed over a hundred men who, come payday, were eager for a drink and a poke without having to make the two day ride to Shakespeare just to get them. Now the mine was almost played out and Olvidados along with it.

"Don't you think you brought too much gun?" Charlie asked. He gestured to the two ten gauge coach guns I had, one in a scabbard tied to my saddle, the other in a sling on my back. They were left over from my time in the shotgun seat. I also had my Colt holstered to my hip, although I wasn't nearly as good with mine as Charlie was with his, which was why I had the two coach guns.

"No such thing," I said.

"Bet you also got that old Marston in your boot," Charlie said.

"I do," I said.

"For a man so reluctant to kill you sure come prepared for it."

"I may be reluctant, but in the event I'd rather it be him than me."

"Amen, brother," Charlie said.

When we got to the mine I fell back behind Charlie and we rode single file down the haul road into the open pit. As we neared the bottom I could see there weren't more than a dozen men working and only one ore cart waiting to be filled. Beside a weather-beaten shack not much bigger than an outhouse there sat a pile of unused shovels and picks.Everybody stopped working to watch us as we rode by. One fella stood back from the others, leaning on a shovel. He was tall, smoking a cheroot and wearing a beat-up bowler hat that looked to be two sizes too small. I figured him for the foreman seeing as how he was doing the least work. Charlie must have figured the same because he rode right up to the man.

"Good afternoon," Charlie said.

"Maybe up top," the man said. "Down here it's hotter than the inside of a buffalo's ass. Plus I got the piles something awful. So don't go telling me how Goddamn good your afternoon is."

Charlie looked back over his shoulder at me. He grinned, then turned back to the man.

"I can tell you ain't one for small talk, so I'll get to the point. Are you the foreman?"

"I am."

"Your name Cullins?"

The foreman's eyes narrowed. "Who's asking?"

"My name is Charlie Brittle, and this here is Owen Ashe." The man glanced in my direction, then back at Charlie. "What do you want?"

Charlie swung down off his horse and stepped right up to the man. The foreman was a good three inches taller and outweighed him by at least sixty pounds, but he seemed to shrink as Charlie got closer.

"What I want is for you to answer my damn question."

The man swallowed, nodded. "I'm Cullins."

"We're looking for your brother Arbo. He's wanted for murder and bank robbery, and we intend to take him back with us."

Cullins didn't hesitate. He jerked his thumb over his shoulder toward the shack.

"Why the hell didn't you just say so," Cullins said. "Sonbitch won't do a lick of work. Been sponging off me since he got here. Pappy always said Arbo would come to no good. One of the few times that old bastard was right."

Just then a weathered looking fella I took to be Arbo leaned out of the door of the shack. One eye was white as snow, and he had teeth that would have made a beaver jealous. He also had a 40-44 revolver in his hand.

Arbo popped off a shot that hit Cullins in the back of the head. Cullin's tiny bowler hat jumped up like it was on a spring, and the lit cheroot shot out of his mouth, bounced off Charlie's shoulder and sent up a little spray of sparks.

"You back stabbin' bastard," Arbo yelled before retreating back inside the shack.

The foreman didn't hear him. His dead eyes stared up at me. Blood poured steadily from the back of his head and ran down into the crevices of the ground he'd worked.

Several of the miners jumped for cover when Arbo fired, but the rest moved toward us. I didn't know if they were coming to the aid of their foreman, or just trying to get a gander at the action. I wasn't going to wait to find out.

I climbed down off my horse and hauled the coach gun from its scabbard. Cradling it like a baby, I took a few steps toward the approaching miners.

"That's close enough boys," I said. "This bitch is not choosy. If I try to shoot one of you her spread will kill three."

That stopped them in their tracks.

Charlie drew his Colt and faced the shack. "Arbo, you are one low down dog. You done killed your own brother."

"We wasn't all that close," Arbo called back.

"You come out now," Charlie said. "Nobody else has to get hurt. If you don't, I'm going to kill you. That's for certain."

"Go kiss a mule's ass." Arbo still didn't show himself.

Charlie fired twice through the wall of the shack.

"Oh, Goddamn," Arbo said.

Arbo stumbled out of the shack clutching at his belly.

He made a halfhearted attempt to raise his gun and Charlie shot him in the face. Arbo fell atop the stack of picks and shovels, and they made an awful clatter as his body rolled down to the ground.

Charlie had a canvas tarp folded up and stashed behind his saddle. I kept watch on the miners while he got the tarp and used it as a winding sheet for Arbo. He tied the sheet in place with rope, then grabbed the body by the legs and drug it toward my horse.

"I don't want that thing riding with me," I said. "You killed him, you haul him."

"Fine," Charlie said. "Next time we bring a damn pack mule."

By the time he got Arbo situated onto the back of his horse, Charlie was breathing hard.

"Thanks for the help," Charlie said.

"I'm handling business over here," I said.

Charlie looked at the miners. "Yeah, they look like a formidable bunch."

I kept the coach gun out and resting across my lap as we started back up the haul road. I wanted to keep it out for the miners to see. I doubted any of them cared a whit about Arbo or his brother, but men can react in violent and unexpected ways when you invade their territory.

"What do we do with him?" One of the miners called out. He pointed at the foreman's body.

"You boys are the ones with the shovels," Charlie said. "Dig a hole and bury him."

THREE

Dottie stood in the doorway of the saloon watching Charlie and me tie our bedrolls behind our saddles. She sipped from a glass of whiskey. From the way she leaned against the frame I could tell she'd had a few.

"That didn't take long," she said.

That same thought had been circling my mind the whole ride back. The decision to hunt a man for money, find him and kill him hadn't taken more than an afternoon. It seemed to me that something like that should have been a more time consuming endeavor. I wasn't sure why I felt that way, but it troubled me nonetheless.

Charlie and I had talked it over. We still had several hours of daylight left and decided it was best to get started on the ride to Shakespeare.

"You paying for all your drinking?" Charlie asked.

"Nope," Dottie said. "You paying me for watching the place?"

"You drink all you want, Dottie," I said.

Dottie gave me a smile.

Charlie glared at me, but didn't say anything.

"You mind if I sleep here while you're gone?" Dottie asked. "Them girls I bunk with smell worse than a dead hog. I wonder sometimes if they'd recognize a bathtub if they saw one."

"For a whore," Charlie said. "You sure got a low opinion of other whores."

Dottie shrugged. "I doubt you hold other bounty hunters in high esteem."I told Dottie she could sleep there.

"Hey, Owen?" Dottie said.

"Yeah, Dottie?" I said.

"Maybe if I do a good enough job running the place while you're gone I could take it up permanent like. Tending bar, I mean."

Dottie's hopeful look was hard to face. The truth was Charlie and I could have ridden away for a week, left the door wide open with a sign out front that said 'free whiskey', and still not had a customer. But admitting that to Dottie meant admitting it to myself.

"That sounds fine," I said.

Dottie smiled. "Really? That's good. I sure would like to leave the poke business behind."

We finished loading up and rode out. Dottie waved, and I waved back. Charlie pretended not to see her.

"I think Dottie's right," I said.

"I would be surprised if that were true," Charlie said. "But just what is it you think she's right about."

"Only bounty hunters I ever met were dirty, back-shooting scum. Not sure how I feel being one of them."

"No different than any other job," Charlie said. "There's right ways and wrong ways to go about it."

"You think we went about this the right way?"

"I do. Arbo Cullins was a murderous bastard. You saw him shoot a man dead right in front of you. Far as I'm concerned he's a perfect example of a man who needed killing."

Charlie went quiet after that, and I could tell that he wasn't interested in discussing it further. He was not a man prone to over thinking, or second guessing himself. If he felt his actions were just, he considered further reflection a waste of time.

We made camp just before dark and had some of the jerky for dinner. Later, as I lay staring up at the endless night sky, unable to sleep, I found myself wishing my mind worked more like Charlie's.

FOUR

We arrived in Shakespeare early the next evening and went directly to the Sheriff's office. The Sheriff's name was Bragg Stanley, and he looked to be in his mid-fifties. He was big and beefy, with a low swaying belly. He wore no hat, and a fringe of lank, gray hair circled his pink, sweaty scalp.

He greeted us with little enthusiasm.

"Did you have to shoot him in the face?" Stanley asked. "You sure made a mess of him."

"He was plenty unappealing even before I shot him," Charlie said.

Charlie had laid the body on the boardwalk in front of Stanley's office. The sheet was pulled back from Arbo's face, and the three of us stood around him.

Through the open door of the office I could see a plain looking room with a cell in the back. In the center of the room a pair of tables had been pushed together to use as desks. A chubby deputy sat on one side, stuffing his face full of fried chicken and mashed potatoes. A half-eaten plate of the same sat on the opposite side. It seemed we had interrupted Stanley's dinner, which probably accounted for his sour mood.

Stanley held the wanted notice in his hand and

looked over it, his lips moving as he read. He knelt down and lifted each of Arbo's eyelids. Satisfied, he stood back up, grunting at the effort.

"Well," Stanley said. "He's got the eye. And them teeth look they was tossed in his mouth from a dice cup. I reckon that's the right man."

"We wouldn't have shot him if he wasn't," I said.

Stanley gave me a scornful look. "It's been done before."

"Not by us," Charlie said. "And now that we all agree on who this fella is, do we get our money?"

"You'll have to wait a bit on that," Stanley said.

I could sense Charlie tensing up, ready for a fight. "How long?"

"Just till the bank opens in the morning," Stanley said.

"We weren't planning on staying overnight," Charlie said.

"And I wasn't planning on staring at a face-shot dead man during dinner," Stanley said. "Looks like we all got surprised."

"No way to get that money tonight?" Charlie asked.

"You think I carry it around in my boot?" Stanley said. "Come back in the morning. And when you do I'll need you to sign some papers, if that ain't too much fucking trouble."

Charlie nodded. "Fine then. We'll be by first thing."

"Fine then," Stanley said. "In the meantime you can take this body to the undertaker. He's getting ripe."

"It's your body now," Charlie said. "Have that deputy take it over. He looks capable."

The deputy looked up when he was mentioned. He wore a dollop of gravy on his chin.

"You are an un-likeable cuss," Stanley said.

Charlie grinned, said, "I have my charms."

"Well, next time bring'em with you," Stanley said.

FIVE

Shakespeare wasn't much of a town, but compared to Olvidados it was a thriving metropolis. Charlie and I put our horses up at the livery, then spent some time wandering around just watching and listening to the people. In Olvidados you could go hours without seeing anybody on the town's single, short street.

I got some strange looks for toting two shotguns around, which amused Charlie no end.

"You sure you wouldn't rather drag a cannon around behind you?" Charlie asked.

"You'll be glad I have'em if we ever need'em," I said.

"That's true enough," Charlie said. "But then you could say the same thing about a cannon."

We found a cafe called Good Eats and went inside. After seeing Stanley's dinner I had a hankering for fried chicken, but it wasn't on the menu. Their dinner selection was limited to ham and beans, boiled mutton, or something called Steak Jamboree. I had the mutton.

Charlie had the Steak Jamboree and when I asked him how it was he said, "You made the right choice, hoss. If Stanley doesn't have our money tomorrow I'm gonna thump him, then come back here and shoot the cook."

There was only one hotel in town. It wasn't anything to crow about, but the promise of a real bed made me feel like it was Christmas day. Charlie was still unhappy about having to spend the night in Shakespeare. It didn't bother me. I was perfectly happy to sleep anywhere that wasn't the ground or a cot in the back of a saloon. We got a pair of rooms and turned in for the night.

I lay awake for a while, pondering this whole bounty hunting business. I'd killed men before, but the act had always been thrust upon me, leaving me no choice. I'd shot and killed two bandits when I rode shotgun. And I'd shot a few and beaten many in some of the rowdier saloons where Charlie and I had worked and first met. But until now I had never sought a man out with the intention of killing him, which is exactly what we'd done. Despite what I'd said to Charlie, I never really expected Arbo to allow himself to be arrested.

After an hour or so of tossing, I finally fell asleep. It was a restless sleep troubled by dreams of bowler hats that smoked cigars and spouted blood from their crowns. At one point in the dream a giant set of teeth, spaced as wide apart as jail bars, floated toward me. Dottie was on the other side of those choppers smiling and calling to me, but I couldn't get past those teeth to reach her.

I woke up fast to the sound of someone pounding on the door of my room. I stumbled out of bed, rubbing at my face, and hastily pulled on my pants. Silly as it had been, I was unsettled by my nightmare.

When I opened the door I saw the fat clerk from the front desk standing in the hall. The clerk's hair was mussed, like he'd been pulled out of bed himself, and he didn't look to be happy about it. Seemed like everybody in this town was a porker with a sour disposition.

"The Sheriff wants to see you downstairs," he said.

"He say what it's about?" I asked.

"He didn't say, and I didn't ask," the clerk said. "Just went through all this with your friend."

Across the hall Charlie stood in the open door of his room. The clerk must have woken him up first. He didn't look any more alert than I was, but he was fully dressed and just putting on his hat.

The clerk stormed away, not waiting for Charlie or me. Charlie waited in the doorway while I finished dressing.

"You think it's about our money?" I asked.

"I figure it is," Charlie said. "One way or another."

SIX

Stanley and his deputy were waiting for us in the lobby. As we came down the stairs they both scowled at us, which looked normal on Stanley, but kind of silly on the cherub faced deputy. At least he'd wiped the gravy off his chin.

"What's this about, Sheriff?" Charlie asked. "I know you didn't open the bank special for us."

Stanley hesitated before answering. He glanced at his deputy, whose scowl had turned into more of a pout.

"I'm gonna have to deputize the two of you," Stanley said. He held out his hand and showed us a pair of stars.

"What for?" I asked.

"Got a situation over at Belle's. Not the sort of thing Hank and I are used to facing."

"I could handle it," Hank said.

"You could get your ass shot off is what you could do," Stanley said. "We ain't gunnies, neither of us. But I'm willing to bet these two been in some sticky situations before."

I could understand the sheriff thinking what he did about Charlie. I'd been riding with him for close to four years, he'd saved my skin a number of times, and I considered him my most trusted friend. But even I couldn't deny there was a sense of impending violence about Charlie. Sometimes being near him was like watching a storm roll in across an open plain. All you could do was hope it changed direction before it swept you up.

Stanley's assessment of me was a surprise. I'd never thought of myself as a gunhand, just a fella whose various jobs often required the application of a gun. Up until now that distinction had always left me feeling comfortable about the things I'd done, but the sheriff's words hung in my head.

"Don't we have some say in the matter of being deputized?" Charlie asked.

"Sure," Stanley said. "And seeing as how Arbo Cullins was shot in the face, I might need to have a marshall come and make an official identification before you get your money. That would only take a week or three."

"You know damn well that was Arbo," Charlie said. "You said it yourself."

"And now I'm having second thoughts," Stanley said. "My old eyes ain't what they used to be."

"But they'll improve some if we help you out." Charlie said.

"Good as glasses," Stanley said.

Charlie took the badges out of Stanley's hand and passed one to me. We pinned them on and stood looking down at our chests for a moment.

"From saloon owner to star packer in one day," Charlie said. "At this rate I'll be president by next week."

SEVEN

Big Bottom Belle's was a whore house that sat out on the edge of town. Like everything else in Shakespeare, it was nicer than what we had back in Olvidados. Belle's was a big, two-story house with a wrap-around porch. A little picket fence went all around the front yard. The place was lit up inside, and with the red curtains in the windows it glowed warmly in the night.

"Bet they charge more than the whores back home in Olvidados," I said.

"Way most of the whores in Olvidados look, they ought to be the ones paying," Charlie said.

There were four horses hitched at the rail in front of Belle's. As we walked by, the nearest one made a snap at Hank's ear and just about got it. Hank did a quick sidestep and bumped into Stanley who shoved him out of the way.

"Even those bastards' horses are mean," Hank said. He rubbed at his ear, like he was thinking on the near miss. As the four of us went through the gate and up the walk, a heavy-set woman in a blue silk robe rushed out the door. She came down the porch steps, then went back up. Then she turned around and did the same thing again, agitated and impatient. She was a big bosomed woman, and the one handed grip she was using to keep the robe closed was not up to the task. Each trip up or down the stairs allowed a little more of her to bounce out and enjoy the night air.

"You sure took your sweet time," the woman said. "Thought they were gonna steal one of my girls before you got back."

"Calm down, Belle," Stanley said. "Nobody's running off with your girls.

"They say they are," Belle said.

"Well, we say they ain't," Hank said, his voice louder than it needed to be.

Stanley gave him a look, and Hank went quiet.

There was a swing on the porch and a man wearing a white shirt and black suspenders sat in it. His head was tilted back and he had his hands over his mouth. When he heard us he sat up and took his hands down. There was blood smeared across the bottom half of his face. I saw he had an unloaded Greener cracked open across his lap.

"They took my thells," the man said. When he spoke he revealed the raw gumline where his front teeth had been shattered.

"Looks like they took your teeth too," Stanley said. "I told you to wait for me to get back."

"Belle thaid to do thomething," the man said. "Tho I did thomething."

"Stop talking," Stanley said. "It hurts to listen to you."

"You thould try it from thith end," the man said.

Stanley left the man sitting there and led us inside. As I passed him by the man eyed the ten gauge in my arms.

"Careful they don't take your thells," he said.

"They won't," I said.

Just inside the door of Belle's there was a hallway going straight ahead. Off to the right was a long staircase leading to the upstairs rooms, and to the left was an open doorway that led into the parlor where customers waited for their turn with a dove. The parlor had several sofas and comfortable looking chairs, and a short bar along the back wall.

There were at least a dozen girls seated around the parlor in various states of undress, and all of them looked nervous as cats. The only customers that I could see were two filthy looking men at the bar. I could smell them both from across the room. They smelled like sweat, piss, and more sweat.

One of the men was thin with a beaky nose and long greasy hair. He wore a dusty overcoat and had a battered top-hat perched crookedly atop his head. A bowie knife hung from his belt. The other man was well over six foot tall and bald as an egg. He wore suspenders with no shirt and had muscles that looked like rocks grinding together under his skin when he moved. I saw he had a Remington Army revolver stuffed into the front of his britches.

Upon seeing us enter, one of the girls sprung from her seat and made a dash for the door. Her path took her past Top-Hat who whirled around and grabbed her by the arm. The girl jerked to a stop and Top-Hat shoved her back toward her chair. She moved back to her place, but didn't sit.

"I told you to wait," Top-Hat said. "I find it annoying to have to repeat myself. I'll be making my choice soon as Zeke gets back down here."

Stanley jerked his head in the direction of the bar, said to Charlie and me, "Other one is upstairs. They been here all night."

"Told'em to leave," Hank said. "But they didn't leave."

"I can see that," I said.

Charlie looked at me. I nodded and moved over so that I could cover the stairs with the ten gauge, but still watch the parlor. I'd left the other shotgun back in my hotel room and I felt about as naked as one of Belle's doves without it.

Charlie moved to the bar on the other side of Top-Hat. Stanley approached Top-Hat and Baldy directly, with Hank trailing behind him. Belle moved over by her girls.

Top-Hat didn't acknowledge us at all. He took a pull from a bottle of whiskey and passed it to Baldy who wasn't quite as comfortable ignoring us. He cut his eyes to the side as he drank. Watching.

"It's time for you boys to skedaddle," Stanley said.

Top-Hat made a show of keeping his back to Stanley. "Well, hello, Sheriff. I didn't think you and that turd of a deputy would have the nerve to come back. I see you had to bring a couple extra turds with you."

Top-Hat slowly turned to look at Charlie as he spoke. Charlie grinned at him, his hand hanging loose by his Colt.

"Time to go," Stanley said. "Get that other one down here and be on your way."

"We paid for a woman," Baldy said. "Didn't we, Abe?"

Top-Hat nodded. "Eli's telling it right, Sheriff."

"You paid for a woman's time," Stanley said. "And your time is up."

"I have decided to take a wife," Abe said. "Matrimony is a big decision, and there are an awful lot of potentiable brides here. More than even I can handle in one night. So my brothers have agreed to help me consider all my options."

"Ain't none of these girls gonna marry any of you dirty pieces of shit," Belle said.

Abe spun on Belle so fast his hat flew off his head and rolled under a table.

"Shut your mouth, sow. I am gonna lift one of these fallen women up from this pit of vileness and show her God's path. But I can't know which one of these filthy whores is the chosen one until we fuck'em all."

"I'll throw your asses out if I have to," Stanley said. He moved forward, as if to grab hold of Abe.

Abe pulled the bowie knife from its sheath with graceful ease. The blade gleamed in the lamplight as he brandished it at Stanley.

"One more step and I'll uncork you," Abe said.

Charlie moved quickly. He reached out and clamped his hand over Abe's knife hand. He twisted and brought the hand up, smacked Abe between the eyes with the edge of his own blade. The skin of Abe's forehead split wide, and blood poured down his face. Abe screamed, and the knife clattered to the floor.

I charged across the parlor as soon as Charlie made his move. Stanley and Hank were focused on Abe and didn't notice Eli fumble for his Remington. He'd just about gotten the gun out of his pants when I swung the ten-gauge and bashed him full in the face with both barrels. Eli bent backwards, and his head bounced off the bar before he slid down to the floor, blood spurting from both nostrils.

I heard a door slam from upstairs and stepped back through the doorway into the hall. A young man with a scraggly beard charged down the steps. He held his pants up with one hand and gripped a Colt in the other.

I brought the shotgun to bear, thumbed back both hammers. I was hoping to discourage him, but he was already committed to a course of action. He brought his gun up, and I let fly with a single barrel.

The blast caught the man under the chin, and the front half of his head disappeared. A good section of the stair rail blew apart as well, driving several large splinters of wood into his chest. The body fell back against the wall, slid sideways, then tumbled down a couple of stairs where it got jammed and hung ass-over-tea-kettle.

For the next few seconds everything was quiet in the whore house.

EIGHT

"**God's wrath will reign** down upon you for this," Abe said. We were outside with the two brothers as they tied the body of the third over the back of his horse. Belle and several of her girls stood on the front porch watching.

We had taken all of their guns, along with Abe's bowie knife. Stanley said he wanted them out of town rather than in a cell, so we had ushered them out the door.

Abe was wearing his top-hat again, but it was mashed to shit from Charlie giving it a good stomping. He had a bandana tied around his forehead to cover up the nasty gash there. A little trickle of blood escaped and ran down the bridge of his nose.

"I ain't looking forward to facing Pa," Eli said. "Zeke was his favorite."

"He was not," Abe said. "Pa loves all his sons equal. Just as God loves all his children equal."

Abe turned and pointed a finger at Charlie and me.

"Except for you sonbitches," Abe said. "God will flay the skin from your bones, then send you to burn in the pits of Hell, and crows shall peck out your eyes."

The blood running down Abe's nose had collectied

into a big fat drop on the tip. That drop waggled back and forth in a distracting manner as he talked. And he talked a lot. Once he'd realized we weren't going to shoot him he started in on his fire and brimstone chatter, and didn't let up.

"Your blood will boil in your veins," Abe said. "And your bones will be ground to dust."

"That's a lot to keep track of," I said. "Is all this before or after the crows have at me?"

"Don't you mock God's wrath," Abe said.

"Only wrath you got to worry about is mine," Charlie said. He held up the bowie knife he'd taken possession of. "It ain't too late for me to bury this between your ribs."

The sight of the knife was enough to stop Abe's talking. He looked to Stanley for help, but the sheriff, consciously or not, had turned things over to Charlie. He hadn't said a word since we'd come outside, and he didn't now.

Seeing that he was well and truly in danger of being skewered by his own knife, Abe motioned for Eli to mount up.

"Sure ain't looking forward to facing Pa," Eli said.

"You already Goddamn said that," Abe said. "Now get Zeke's horse, and let's go."

Eli tied a lead onto the horse with the body on it and the group rode off. Stanley, Hank, Charlie and I all moved out into the street. We watched them until there wasn't anything to see but night.

Then Abe's voice came shouting back at us from far away in the dark. "Abraham Scault will have his revenge." A moment of silence, then faintly, "You sonbitches."

Charlie turned to Stanley, his jaw tight. "You never said those lowlifes were the Scaults."

"I didn't know," Stanley said.

Charlie stared at him. "You knew. That's why you needed us to do your job for you. You cowardly bastard."

"Watch your mouth," Hank said, and he grabbed hold of Charlie's arm when he said it.

Charlie pulled away and pounded a fist into Hank's jaw hard enough to give me a headache just from seeing it. The deputy went to his knees, sort of wobbled a bit, then sat down like he needed to think on things a while.

"I knew they were part of Hurnen Scault's bunch," Stanley said. "But I didn't know they were his damn sons. I swear I didn't."

Hurnen Scault. I couldn't recall hearing the name before. I was certain Charlie had never mentioned him.

Charlie pulled the star off of his shirt. He reached over and pulled mine off as well, then threw both of them on the ground at Stanley's feet.

"You should have told me up front, damn you," Charlie said. "Would have made a difference."

"How's that?" Hank got slowly to his feet. He rubbed at his jaw. "You mean you would have backed down if you'd known who they were?"

"No," Charlie said. "I would've killed them all and told God they got lost in the desert."

NINE

On the walk back to the hotel I asked Charlie about Hurnen Scault.

"Is he some kind of outlaw?" I asked.

"He's an outlaw alright," Charlie said. "But that description ain't sufficient. He and his bunch been living in the desert for years. Scault runs some kind of refuge out there. If you're on the run from the law, he'll take you in if you pay his price. But from what I hear only the lowest of the low are willing to ride with Scault, live like he lives. They prey on travelers. Rob and kill 'em. Do worse to the women. They're a scourge, is what they are."

"And I killed one of his sons," I said.

"Looks that way," Charlie said.

"And Stanley just sent the other two home to tell their daddy," I said.

"Yep," Charlie said.

"Think he might feel raw about it?" I asked. "Want to settle scores?"

"It's something he's known for," Charlie said. "From what I heard, he's crazy with religion. Scault believes he and his kin are chosen by God to carry out His will. Thinks any horrible thing they do is ace-high with the almighty. And it sounds like his boy Abraham is a true believer."

"So you think they'll come straight at us?" I asked. "Or are we gonna have to watch our backs for the foreseeable future?"

"With this bunch," Charlie said. "I would not expect to see them coming. Back-shooting snakes, every one. What we got in our favor right now is that they don't know we don't normally lay our heads in Shakespeare."

"That buys us some time," I said.

"It does," Charlie said. "Those boys got a long ride ahead of them. Gives us a chance to figure out our next move."

"Be good to have a plan if Scault comes looking for us," I said.

"When," Charlie said.

"You that dead certain?" I asked.

Charlie didn't say anything. He just kept walking, and I kept following him in the dark.

TEN

Charlie and I slept in the next morning. We didn't figure Stanley for an early riser and neither of us wanted to be sitting around twiddling our thumbs while we waited on him to fetch our money from the bank. It was after ten when we finally got up and headed for the Sheriff's office.

The door to the office wouldn't open and nobody answered. We went back to the cafe where we'd eaten the night before and had eggs, bacon and coffee. Their breakfast was a damn sight better than their dinner. Charlie was too annoyed with waiting on Stanley to enjoy the meal, so I finished his.

We met up with Stanley on the street as we were headed back to his office.

"Thought you boys would be on your way by now," Stanley said.

"Not without our money," Charlie said.

Stanley looked at him funny.

"Hank was supposed to get that for you first thing," Stanley said.

"We ain't seen the deputy," Charlie said.

"Did you go to the office?" Stanley asked.

"No," Charlie said. "We just stared at the sun till we

went blind. Course we went to the office. It's locked up tight."

"That door's not supposed to be locked," Stanley said. "Hank and I trade off sleeping in the back room. That way one of us is on duty all the time. Did you knock?"

"I knocked," Charlie said.

"That Hank's a sound sleeper," Stanley said. "Did you knock hard?"

Charlie didn't answer.

We got to the office and Stanley tried the door.

"Damn thing won't open," Stanley said.

"That's a surprise," I said.

Stanley pounded on the door. We waited a moment. Stanley pounded again.

"Open up, Hank," Stanley said. "Open this door. You hear me?"

"The whole town hears you," Charlie said. "Don't you have a key?"

"Never needed a key," Stanley said. "Damn door's not supposed to be locked."

Charlie looked at me and shook his head.

He pushed Stanley aside, reared back and kicked the door. It moved a little, but didn't open. Charlie kicked it again and it opened a few inches and stopped. He handed me his hat, then pushed at the door until it opened enough to poke his head inside.

"It's Hank," Charlie said. "He's lying up against the door."

Charlie laid his shoulder against the door and pushed. The door moved slowly and steadily. When it was opened wide enough Charlie slipped through. He pulled Hank out of the way and we all went inside. Charlie took his hat back and we gathered around Hank.

The deputy was curled up on his side laying in a pool of blood. When we turned him over I could see that one of his eyes had been gouged out, his nose cut off. He'd been scalped and cut all over. His pants were down around his knees, and he was cut up between his legs in a way that gave me the urge to cup myself with my hands.

The inside of the office smelled like a slaughter house. There was blood all over the table where I'd seen Hank eating his dinner the night before. It was smeared all around on the top, dripped down and pooled up thick and sticky on the seat of a chair. Flies buzzed around, happy as flies get. It looked like Hank had gotten himself off the table after they'd finished cutting on him, tried to get outside, and he passed out up against the door. Stanley knelt down beside the deputy. He wrestled him around for a minute trying to pull Hanks pants up, but all he managed to do was get himself covered in blood. He kept saying "Goddamn. Goddamn."

Hank looked dead, but then he let out a low moaning sound that made my skin crawl.

"I'll get the doc," Stanley said. The sheriff started to lumber to his feet.

Charlie put a hand on his shoulder.

"Just stay by him," Charlie said. "Doc ain't gonna make any difference."

Hank made that moaning sound again. After a second I figured out he was trying to say something. We all leaned closer.

"I didn't tell'em," Hank said.

"Didn't tell them what?" Charlie asked. "What are you talking about?"

Hank made a hissing sound that I took to be a laugh. "Didn't tell those bastards you were at the hotel. Said you went home. Back to Olvidados."

Hank began to tremble. His one eye rolled around in his head for a moment, then focused on Stanley.

"Know what I think?" Hank asked.

"What's that?" Stanley asked.

Hank kept giving Stanley that one-eyed stare, his mouth hanging open. We all waited. After a few seconds we realized the deputy was gone, along with whatever it was he'd been thinking.

ELEVEN

Stanley insisted on getting us our money right away. Even before he sent for the undertaker. Said we were bad luck, and he wanted us out of town. I didn't remind him that it was his bright idea to have Charlie and me deal with the Scaults. Didn't seem appropriate.

Charlie and I figured the brothers had circled around after they left Belle's, watched the Sheriff's office from a distance. Once they were sure Hank was alone, they snuck up on him while he was sleeping, held him down and did their nasty business.

The folks at the bank were awful nervous about handing the money over to Stanley, him being covered in blood the way he was. It probably didn't help that Charlie and I were standing there with him, armed the way we were. The teller called another teller over, that teller fetched the manager over, then the manager had a few words with Stanley. They finally gave him the money and he gave it to us. That thousand dollars didn't seem like as much as it had when we'd started out.

It was well past noon by the time we started on the ride back to Olvidados. There were no clouds, and the sun beat down on us from a sky so blue it made your eyes ache to look at it.

We discussed the Scault situation. "Way they did Hank seems to fit what you said about them not coming at us straight on," I said.

"It does," Charlie said.

"Stanley said they took Hank's gun," I said.

"And the Winchesters from the office," Charlie said.

"Could be planning to ambush us on the way," I said.

"If Hank told them we'd already left," Charlie said. "Then they think we're ahead of them."

"If Hank was telling the truth," I said. "Not to speak ill of the dead, but the deputy was a puffed up rooster. Wouldn't put it past him to use his last breath to brag on himself. Could be what he really did was tell them where we were headed, give them the chance to prepare a surprise along the way."

Charlie rode along and thought on that for a bit.

"Nope," Charlie said. "Don't believe he did."

"So you think Hank lied to the Scault brothers," I said. "Thought he was helping us by telling them we'd left town, so they wouldn't know we're trailing along behind."

"Yep," Charlie said.

"But what he really did was tell them where we live," I said. "Taking away the one advantage we had."

"Yep," Charlie said. "That about hits the nail on the head."

"Least he was consistent," I said. "Useless to the bitter end."

We rode along a bit more, considering things.

I asked, "You think they'll head back and get the rest of their bunch? Or lay in wait once they see we're not in Olvidados?"

"That's the question," Charlie said.

"Guess we'll find out when we get there," I said.

"Guess we will," Charlie said.

We rode as long as we could that first day, but finally had to stop around sundown and rest the horses. Way we figured, the Scaults had either already reached Olvidados, or they'd headed on back to their hidey-hole in the desert and would poke their heads out at some point in the future.In all our talk about the topic, Charlie and I never figured there was a third possibility. It was one that proved worse than anything we'd considered.

TWELVE

We smelled the smoke, but missed the fire.

It was going on noon when we topped the hill on the edge of town. Down below a haze hung in the air like an early morning mist, but dirty and gray. Through the haze I could see there was a wagon in the street in front of the Horseshoe Saloon, and there were several people milling about. That was a bustle of activity for Olvidados. As we rode closer I saw there were three bodies in the back of the wagon, and the bartender from the Horseshoe, a skinny fella named Waller, was loading a fourth. When he saw us approaching he left off loading the body and walked out to meet us.

"Wasn't anything we could do," he said. "Them boys meant business."

Charlie looked down at him from horseback.

"Okay," Charlie said. "Mind telling me what we're talking about."

"They rode in at first light," Waller said. "They shot Lucius and the two Dans."

"For no reason?" Charlie asked.

"Not much of one," Waller said. "Asked us where you were. Lucius asked'em why they wanted to know and a big, bald fella shot him dead. Then he shot the two Dans. Man in a mashed top-hat said that was just so we knew he meant business. Then Rufo told'em we knew they meant business when they shot Lucius. Said shooting the two Dans was redundant. Ol' Rufo liked to use them big words."

Charlie glanced at the four bodies.

"I'm guessing they shot him too," Charlie said.

"Shot him too," Waller said.

Lucius ran the dirty fly-trap across the street from the Horseshoe that went by the dandied up name of The Royal Chandelier Drinking Establishment. Dan Jones and Dan Strunk had been miners in the past, but drunks since I'd known them. They split their time between the Royal Chandelier and the Horseshoe. Rufo worked for Waller, and that's all I knew about him. Between them they made up a significant portion of the Olvidados population.

While Waller parsed the story out to Charlie in dribs and drabs the wind kicked up. As the haze slowly lifted I peered ahead, trying to see down to the other end of the street to our place. I had a sick feeling stirring in my stomach.

"After all that shooting I hope you went ahead and told them we were out of town," Charlie said.

"We didn't know you were out of town," Waller said. "We saw Dottie down there and figured you were there like usual." I put the heels to my horse and it took off at a run. Behind me I heard Charlie say, "Aw, damn it."

The haze over Olvidados came from the smoldering

remains of our saloon. It had burned up like dry kin-
dling. The only thing remaining was one of our chairs
from the porch that now lay in the street. The fact
that our place was set off a ways from the rest of the
buildings was probably the only reason the whole town
hadn't burned.

I got off my horse and moved as close as the pile of
hot embers would let me. I looked for Dottie. Hoped
I wouldn't see her. I felt Charlie step up beside me.

"What's this," Charlie said.

Charlie went and fetched the chair out of the street
and brought it over. On the seat someone had scratched
words deep into the wood.

Looks like I got my wife after all

Go too hell

I stared off past our place, through the haze and
out at the sun-baked land beyond. I pictured Dottie
with the Scaults. I wondered if she was hurt, if she
was scared.

"I know what you're thinking," Charlie said. "And
just get it out of your mind. They got half a day's ride
on us."

"She was working for us," I said. "That means she
was our responsibility."

"The Hell it does," Charlie said. "She didn't really
work for us, you were just humoring her."

"She was working for us," I said.

Charlie threw the chair into the smoking wreckage. He spit on the ground.

"If she'd stayed whoring she wouldn't have got herself into this fix," Charlie said.

I took the reins of my horse and turned back toward the other end of town.

"I didn't want her around here anyway," Charlie said. "I don't feel any responsibility for no stolen dove." I walked back toward the Horseshoe. After a minute I heard Charlie come alongside, our horses walking between us.

"Need to pick up a few supplies," I said.

I heard Charlie say, "Yep."

"Heading out right after," I said.

I heard Charlie say, "Yep."

"Then we're going to find Dottie, and kill the bastards that took her," I said.

I heard Charlie sigh, and say, "Yep."

THIRTEEN

Charlie didn't know precisely where the Scaults went to ground, only that it was deep in the desert. He said he knew a man who could help us find them, and then he said nothing more about it for the next few days.

The ride was hot, slow, and ugly. The further west we went the more brown everything turned. The Ocotillo was in bloom, and it got so my eyes sought out the red flowers just to remind me that the whole world didn't look the color of sand.

On the third day our route took us onto a rocky trail and we followed that. It was almost sundown when we came to a dirty, no-name village made up of half a dozen buildings assembled from clay and scrap wood. I could sense hostile eyes staring out from the shadows of the windowless shacks as we rode by.

A black dog passed us going the opposite direction. He was so skinny his ribs showed, and he growled at me when I looked at him. I got the feeling that was the friendliest greeting we were likely to get in this place.

The last shack in the line had a hitch rail out front and appeared to be a worse attempt at a saloon than our own. It had no door, and only half of a rusted tin roof. The other half was open to the elements. We stopped, got down and tied our horses.

"Your friend in here?" I asked. "The one who can help us find the Scaults?"

"Ain't exactly a friend," Charlie said. "It's more complicated than that. And you better take one of the shotguns in with you."

"Always planned to," I said.

The inside of the saloon would have made a shithouse rat feel house proud. The place smelled of coal oil and man sweat. The uneven dirt floor sloped to the back where the other half of the tin roof lay in a collapsed pile. There was only one table, and it was occupied by three men silently sharing a bottle. All three watched us closely as we entered.

Charlie went to the dry, warped plank that served as the bar. A dark haired man with a widow's peak got up from the table and walked around behind it. The man wore a white, band collared shirt that didn't appear to have been cleaned since the wool came off the sheep. He looked at us, but he didn't speak.

I stood with my back against the bar, cradling the shotgun and meeting the stares of the two men still at the table. Not challenging, just letting them know I was aware of them.

"Looking for Bodaway," Charlie said.

"Don't know who that is," the bartender said.

"Yeah you do," Charlie said.

"He don't come in here no more," the bartender said.

"Yeah he does," Charlie said. "Tell him Charlie Brittle was here."

"Why would I do that?" the bartender asked.

"Because," Charlie said. "If he finds out I was here, and you didn't tell him, he'll probably slit your throat."

The bartender nodded. "Guess you know Bodaway."

"Guess I do," Charlie said.

"Don't I get a tip for my trouble?" the bartender asked.

"Yeah," Charlie said. "Wash that Goddamn shirt."

FOURTEEN

We rode up onto a rocky ridge overlooking the village and made camp. I made a small fire to cook some beans and coffee over.

"So how are we gonna find your friend now?" I asked.

"Bodaway will find us," Charlie said. "And I already told you, he ain't my friend."

It was a hot night, so after we ate and put our bedrolls down I went to put the fire out.

"Leave it be," Charlie said.

"Why?" I asked.

"So it'll draw the attention of our visitors," Charlie said.

"Bodaway?" I asked.

"I'm guessing it's those two from the saloon," Charlie said. "Bodaway's probably watching from somewhere right now, hoping they kill us. Then he won't have to do me the favor he knows I'm gonna ask of him. Plus, it'll save him the trouble of having to kill me later."

"If he wants to kill you, why the Hell would he do you a favor," I asked.

"That's Bodaway for you," Charlie said.

"Your answers are about as clear as mud," I said.

"I told you it was complicated," Charlie said.

He motioned for me to follow him and we went off a ways and crouched behind a couple of jagged boulders stacked one on another. Charlie held a hand to his lips. I went quiet, although I doubt it would have mattered. The two men who approached our camp were so drunk they couldn't have snuck up on us if we were dead. We could hear them tromping up the trail before we ever saw them. I didn't bother to ask how Charlie knew they'd be coming.

"How you know them two got any money," One of the men said. He had a deep voice, and his attempt at a whisper carried louder than if he'd been singing.

"Don't matter," said the other one. "That shotgun and them horses are worth something. If they got pocket money that's just gravy."

"Rivers is gonna be mad we cut him out," Deep Voice said.

"To Hell with Rivers," the other one said.

They came into view and passed right by where Charlie and I were waiting. Just like he said, it was the two from the cantina. One of them stumbled on some loose rocks and the other one caught him.

"Watch it," Deep Voice said. "You might wake'm up."

Charlie and I looked at each other, then stepped out from behind the boulders. Charlie had his Colt out, and I held my shotgun leveled at them.

"Stop," I said.

The two men stopped, raised their hands.

Charlie glanced at me, irritated.

"We oughtta shoot both of you idiots right now," I said. "But I'm gonna give you two a chance. Turn around, go back where you came from, and don't let me see you again."

"Okay," Deep Voice said. "We'll go. Won't we Hobb?"

He nudged Hobb with an elbow and the two of them turned around as if to leave.

"Yeah," Hobb said. "We're going alright."

The two exchanged looks. I guess they were drunk enough to think that with their backs to us we couldn't see what they were doing. That's the only way I can explain what happened next.

As they were telling us how they were going to leave, their hands went slowly to their guns. They didn't hurry at all, didn't give any indication they foresaw the slightest possibility of an unfavorable outcome.

"Hold it," I said. "Just hold it right there."

I couldn't believe what I was watching. Their hands settled, gripped, and began the slowest draws I'd ever seen.

"Goddamnit," I said. "Stop that."

Charlie looked at me, shook his head in disbelief.

He shot both men dead, then went and poured the last of the coffee over the campfire to put it out.

FIFTEEN

In the dark we rolled the two bodies off the ridge. It was about a thirty foot drop, and the sound they made when they hit the rocks below made my stomach turn. It troubled me to think of them laying out there, just waiting to be buzzard food. Charlie wasn't bothered by it at all.

"Buzzard's gotta eat too," Charlie said. "Those two made their choice."

"You're right," I said. "If they hadn't been so damn stupid they'd still be alive."

Charlie was silent, but I could tell something was troubling him. We settled in for the night, and I was just on the edge of sleep when Charlie's voice woke me.

"That ain't it," Charlie said.

"Hm?" I said.

"They ain't dead because they were stupid," Charlie said. "Although they were dumber than a coal bucket."

"They were dumb to try and draw on us when we had'em cold," I said.

"Yes, they were," Charlie said. "But they were dead the moment they snuck into our camp with the intention of robbing us. I never had no intention of sending those two back just so they could make another try later. I only waited because you seemed to have a play in mind. Otherwise I would have shot them the moment they stepped into the light."

"Well," I said. "They're dead now, so I don't see what it matters."

"It matters because of where we're going," Charlie said. "And what we're planning to do."

"We're going to get Dottie," I said.

"We are," Charlie said. "And we're also going to kill every damn Scault we see, and every man jack who rides with them. I'm concerned about your commitment to the matter."

"You think I'm scared?" I asked.

"Course not," Charlie said. "But most of the situations we've faced have come with a choice. The men we've been up against could walk away, or make a move. I'm worried when the time comes you're still gonna be offering that choice."

"I've killed before, Charlie," I said.

"Not like this," Charlie said. "When we get this thing started, you're gonna need to be in your gun mind. You got to become an instrument of destruction with no conscience, no thoughts except killing everything that crosses your path. That's the only way we're gonna live through this."

I was silent for a moment, then I said, "I can do that."

"Gun mind," Charlie said.

"I heard you the first time," I said. "I can do it."

"Good," Charlie said, and then he rolled over and went to sleep.

SIXTEEN

I woke to the sight of an Apache crouched beside my head holding a mean looking bone-handled knife in his hand. My heart broke into a gallop, but I stayed frozen where I lay.

"Morning, snoozy," the Apache said.

He used the knife to cut a hunk from the jerky in his other hand. He ate the jerky and grinned at me as he chewed. I smelled coffee, and my heart began to slow. It seemed unlikely that an Apache out for my scalp would bother to brew up a pot of coffee before he set to cutting.

"Bodaway?" I asked.

The Apache nodded.

"You're no fun," Bodaway said.

Charlie came over and handed me a tin cup full of coffee.

"I told you he wouldn't scream," Charlie said.

Bodaway shrugged.

He wasn't dressed like I would expect an Apache to dress. He wore a brown suit, with his pants tucked into high boots. Instead of a hat he wore a bandana, and his long black hair hung down in back almost to his waist.

"You speak good English," I said.

"Why do white men always say that?" Bodaway asked. "If your horse started speaking English I could understand the surprise."

"It was a compliment," I said.

"Not to me," Bodaway said. "You know how I learned? When I was little I got hauled away to one of those schools that teaches the Apache out of you. I worked hard, learned the language real well. Wanted to be sure when I told a white man to kiss my ass I was saying it properly."

"Didn't mean to hit a sore spot," I said.

"Everything's a sore spot with Bodaway," Charlie said.

"Kiss my ass," Bodaway said. "Both of you."

Bodaway went on eating his jerky. Charlie refilled my cup with coffee, poured himself some and even gave a cup to Bodaway, who accepted politely, as if having breakfast with men he hated was an ordinary thing.

"So I hear the Scaults took your woman," Bodaway said.

"She's not my woman," I said.

Bodaway looked at Charlie. "Your woman?"

Charlie shook his head. "I don't even like her that much."

"Who is she then?" Bodaway asked.

"Just a whore who spends her days in our saloon," Charlie said.

"She's my friend," I said.

"So you're fucking her," Bodaway said.

Charlie and I both shook our heads.

Bodaway chewed his jerky and thought for a moment.

"Let me get it straight," Bodaway said. "Nobody is fucking her, Charlie doesn't like her, I don't even know her, and I don't like either one of you. But together we're supposed to go kill a whole lot of men to get her back."

"That's about the size of it," Charlie said.

Bodaway laughed long and hard. He slipped the last bite of jerky in his mouth and stood up.

"White men are crazy," Bodaway said.

"But you will help," Charlie said.

"Yes," Bodaway said. "And then we're even."

"Then we're even," Charlie said.

"Good," Bodaway said. "Because then I'll be free to kill you."

"You'll be free to try," Charlie said.

I sipped at my coffee and watched Bodaway closely. Both my shotguns lay on my left side. I wondered if I could reach one in time if he tried anything.

Bodaway, as if he were reading my thoughts, pointed his knife down at me, smiled and said, "I bet I'll have to kill you too, snoozy."

SEVENTEEN

Bodaway told us we would reach the Scaults by nightfall if we made good time, so we loaded up and rode out. Charlie and I rode side by side while Bodaway rode a good distance ahead. It was clear that our company was an annoyance to him.

I watched him, sitting straight and tall on his paint, never pausing to drink or rest. He never showed the slightest hint of discomfort. Bodaway rode with his Yellow Boy resting on his shoulder. From time to time the sunlight would strike the copper receiver that gave the rifle its nickname, and the glare would damn near blind me. I thought he might be doing it on purpose.

The terrain grew more desolate and inhospitable the deeper we rode into the desert, and it began to have a strong effect on my thinking. I was not normally a worrier, but after a few hours of barren rocks and hot sun I'd conjured all sorts of possible betrayals on Bodaway's part.

"Are you sure we can trust him?" I asked Charlie.

"He'll keep his word," Charlie said.

"And after?" I asked.

"He'll keep his word," Charlie said.

"Meaning he'll try to kill you," I said.

"He says he owes me a life and a death," Charlie said. "This trip to get Dottie back is the life. Once that's squared, damn right he'll try to kill me. And you, if you try to stop him. Which I damn well expect you to do."

"Is he going to be much help when the shooting starts?" I asked.

"Let me put it this way," Charlie said. "If I was to order a dozen mean sonbitches, and they only sent me Bodaway, I would not feel cheated."

"So how did you get on his bad side?" I asked.

Charlie was silent for a moment, then said "I believe that's a story for another day. There's a lot in my past I'm not proud of. If I was Bodaway, I'd probably want to kill me too."

I watched Bodaway up ahead, riding silently, sitting tall. It was strange to think no matter how well things turned out when we faced the Scaults, at least one of us was certain to die in this desert.

EIGHTEEN

It was a little past noon when we met the dead man.

Bodaway had disappeared over a rocky hill, and when Charlie and I caught sight of him again his horse was stopped beside a dead mule. Bodaway was off his horse and kneeling down by the mule. When we got closer I saw there was a man lying on the ground with his head propped up against the mule's back. The air around them smelled foul, like either man or mule had emptied their bowels.

Charlie and I dismounted and went and stood behind Bodaway. The man looked up at us with relief. If he thought we could do anything for him he was bound for disappointment. He was lungshot, and gutshot, and taking quick little breaths.

"Well, hello there," the man said.

He had to take a few gulps of air, then said, "How are you boys doing?"

"Better than you, it appears," Charlie said.

"Hell," the man said. "This mule's doing better than me. I was just telling your friend here...about the rascals who killed me."

"What did they look like?" Charlie asked.

"Oh, ugly and dirty," the man said. "One of 'em

wore... a top-hat looked like a fat lady sat on it... Other one was bald...had a broken nose. And they had a woman with'em... riding a horse with a dead man loaded on it. Had a gag in her mouth and her hands tied."

"Sounds like the fellas we're looking for," Charlie said.I was relieved to hear that Dottie was still alive, and that Bodaway was leading us in the right direction.

"You the one broke that fella's nose?" the man asked Charlie.

"I did that," I said.

"But I did stomp the other one's hat," Charlie said. "We aim to kill'em both. I hope that's some consolation to you."

"It's not," the man said. "But I appreciate the thought."

"Why did they shoot you?" I asked.

"They said my mule was ugly," the man said. "So they shot it, and laughed about it. I protested, and the bald one got down and hit me in the stomach. Caused me to mess myself, in case you boys hadn't noticed."

"We noticed," Charlie said. "Just didn't want to embarrass you by mentioning it."

"I'm beyond embarrassment," the man said. "Any-way, that's the reason the one in the hat shot me. Said I smelled. Figure he was gonna shoot me anyway, that just gave him an excuse."

"You're right about that," Charlie said. "He's a bad

one." The man was quiet for a minute, just breathing. Blood trickled from the corners of his mouth.

"I hate this place," the man said. "It's ugly as sin... and hotter than six Indians in a wool blanket."

Talking was growing more difficult for him.

"Want some water?" Charlie asked.

The man shook his head.

"This is getting... mighty uncomfortable... They took my gun... I was hoping maybe one of you could..." The man pointed his index finger and put it against his temple.

"I'll do it," Bodaway said.

The man gave Bodaway a wary look.

"You seem awful anxious," the man said. "Is it because I said that thing about the wool blanket?"

Bodaway didn't answer.

"You won't scalp me afterwards?" the man asked.

"No," Bodaway said.

Bodaway held his hand out to Charlie. Charlie gave him his Colt.

"What's your name?" I asked.

"What does it matter," the man said. "I'll be nobody in a second. Nobody... dead in the middle of nowhere... with a mess in my britches. Not the ending I imagined for myself. But I guess I ain't the first to say that."

Bodaway pressed the barrel of the Colt to the man's head, just behind his ear.

"So long boys," the man said. "To Hell with all this."

I looked at the sky just as Bodaway pulled the trigger.

The sound of the shot carried far in that barren place. Bodaway gave the Colt back to Charlie. We mounted up and left the man and his mule behind.

NINETEEN

"I believe we're being followed," I said.

We were a couple hours away from the dead man when I thought I saw riders behind us. They were still a ways off but approaching fast.

"Yep," Charlie said. "Been getting closer for a while now."

"You didn't think to mention them?" I asked.

"Thought you knew," Charlie said.

"Who do you think they are?" I asked.

"If I had to guess," Charlie said. "I'd say they're from that dirt hole we stopped at yesterday. Those two I shot were talking about a fella. Think the name was Rivers."

"You think they followed us all the way out here just to rob us?" I asked.

"It's what they do," Charlie said. "What little we got is more than they got. And they want it."

I watched for a while, trying to figure out how many men were on their way. After a minute I determined there were six riders. I turned to call out to Bodaway and saw his horse was running full out. A rocky hillside lay in the distance and he was heading for its cover as fast as he could.

"I guess his help only extends to the Scaults," I said. Charlie didn't answer.

"Do we follow him?" I asked. "I don't much like being out in the open like this."

"If they have a rifle they'll pick us off before we get very far," Charlie said. "And if they don't they'll have to get a lot closer before they make a move."

"So what do we do?" I asked.

"We wait," Charlie said. "And hope they don't have a rifle."

I pulled one of the coach guns from its scabbard, thumbed back both hammers and rested it across my lap while we waited. The men slowed their horses to a walk as they got closer, then stopped altogether about thirty yards away, apparently surprised to see us just waiting there for them. After a minute or so of talking amongst themselves they resumed their approach with one of them leading the way. He stopped a few feet from us, the other five gathered in a cluster behind him, passing a bottle among them.

The men were a filthy lot. Unshaven, their clothes ragged and full of holes. The lead man had a pair of matching Colts with ivory grips tucked into his pants. They were expensive looking, and I had to think they were stolen off of another traveller who'd had the misfortune to meet him.

"Hello," the man said. "Spare some water for some fellow travellers?"

Neither Charlie nor I spoke. I figured if one of us

reached for a canteen, that was when they would make their move. Our failure to answer seemed to confuse the man.

"Are you deaf?" the man asked. "I say, we're parched. Can you share a little water?"

When we still didn't answer the man leaned over and spit a stream of thick brown tobacco juice onto the ground. His lips twisted into an unkind smile, and he rested a hand on the butt of one of his Colts. The other men seemed to sense the change in the air. They stopped passing the bottle around and sat at attention, waiting for the thing to happen.

"Your name Rivers?" Charlie asked.

This surprised the man.

"Why, yes it is," the man said. "How did you..."

Charlie drew and shot Rivers in the throat. Rivers gagged and choked. He forgot all about his Colts and used both hands to try and stop the blood pouring steadily from the ragged hole.

As Rivers fell from his horse I raised the coach gun and let go with one barrel at the man directly behind him. He caught it in the chest, was knocked sideways off his horse and I immediately fired the second barrel at the man behind him. It hit him in the face, knocked him out of his saddle. The rider beside him took some shot in his shoulder. He didn't go down though, and he held his gun in his other hand. I went for my Colt, knowing I wasn't going to make it. The man jerked as a red hole appeared in his chest, and I heard the crack of Bodaway's rifle.

Charlie had been firing the whole time, and now that I had the chance to notice I saw one man dead on the ground. Another was just as dead but his foot had gotten hung up in a stirrup, and his horse had bolted. I watched him bounce and scrape and stir up dust as his horse headed for the horizon.

I heard Bodaway ride up behind me.

"You sure made yourself scarce," I said.

"Not so scarce I couldn't save your hide," Bodaway said.

"Seemed like you were more interested in saving your own," I said.

Bodaway reined his horse close to mine and pulled back the flap of one of his saddle bags. I saw half a dozen sticks of dynamite inside.

"Didn't want a stray bullet hitting these," Bodaway said. "But maybe I should ride real close to you the rest of the way. Would that make you feel safer?"

"No," I said. "You go on like you have been."

Bodaway grinned and nodded. He turned his horse and rode back out, leading us by a good distance. Charlie and I fell in behind him.

"Did you know he had that dynamite?" I asked.

"Bodaway always has dynamite," Charlie said. "His name means fire maker, and he lives up to it."

"Here I thought he was afraid," I said.

"He was," Charlie said. "He was afraid of getting blowed up."

It occurred to me then that none of us had so much as mentioned the men we'd just shot. There was something about this land that seemed to make the killing easier. We were leaving a trail of bodies like bread crumbs all the way to the Scaults.

TWENTY

It was sunset when we arrived at the Scault's hide-away. There was a stillness in the air, and the sky was streaked blood-red when Bodaway stopped us. We were riding up an incline toward what appeared to be a sheer rock wall. "This is it," Bodaway said.

Charlie and I looked at our surroundings, then at Bodaway.

"I don't see a trail, or a cave," I said. "Are we supposed to climb?"

"The entrance is hidden," Bodaway said. "But I think we need to figure out our plan before we go charging in there."

"You know the place better than we do," Charlie said. "What do you think?"

"Getting in will be easy enough," Bodaway said. "They know me. I've guided plenty of others here before. Rivers tried for months to get me to lead him here, but he never wanted to pay me. Bet now he wishes he had."

"You mean to tell me you work for the Scaults?" I asked.

"I work for the men who pay me to guide them here," Bodaway said. "Just like I'm working for you."

I didn't like being lumped in with the scum who would ride with the Scaults. But I bit my lip.

"So you can get us in," Charlie said. "Provided Abe and Eli don't see us, we should be free to look for Dottie."

"Then what?" I asked.

"I think we'll have to figure that out as we go," Charlie said.

Bodaway nodded. He turned his horse and rode further up the incline. We followed, even though I still couldn't see any kind of an entrance.

Just about the time the ground grew steep enough to worry me, Bodaway reined his horse around and started back down the incline, this time at a slight angle. Charlie and I did the same, and when we did I saw an opening in the wall that hadn't been there before.

The wall was an illusion. If you were riding straight at it, or even coming at it sideways, it looked like a sheer rock face. But if you came at it from downhill, at an angle, you could see that it was two overlapping walls of rock.

The entrance was barely wide enough for a horse and rider to fit through. Then there was a turn and we were riding through a pass with steep cliffs on either side. A minute later we came out into the Scault camp.

It was like being in a box canyon with four sides instead of three. The camp was spread out over at least five acres, with tents and lean-tos scattered all around without any sense of order. Off to one side there was a deep indentation in the rock that was blocked off by planks that served as a corral. Men milled about in front of their flimsy living quarters. I counted twenty heads, and that was just the ones out in the open. The place was noisy, and smelled of human and animal waste.

At the far end of the camp was a ramshackle cabin assembled from scrap wood. It had a low roof, and was built right up against the rock so it only needed three walls. A cross made of lashed together bones was stuck up on the roof and leaned a bit, as if pushed by a strong wind. In front of the shack a man tended a bonfire. Even from this distance I could tell the man was Eli.

As we entered the camp I saw a man with a shotgun sitting lookout from up on a high rock. The man climbed down and came to meet us.

"Bodaway," the man said.

"Glenn," Bodaway said. "Brought a couple men."

"I see that," Glenn said. "I told you we were full up last time you were here."

"Hurnen's going to want these two," Bodaway said. "I guarantee it."

"He might," Glenn said. "But the old man's busy right now. Got himself married again. Pretty little thing. He's preaching at her right now. No telling how long that'll go on. Gonna be a wedding feast later."

"I thought it was Abe getting married," I said.

Bodaway gave me a hateful look, and I realized I might have just gotten us all killed.

"Abe thought so too," Glenn said. "But the old man

took a shine to the girl. Said it was his right as head of the family. Say, how did you hear about it anyway?"

"You know how Abe likes to talk," I said.

It must have been the right thing to say, because Glenn laughed.

"Yeah," Glenn said. "That boy can yammer. Not so much right now though, after the beating Hurnen laid on him. Abe's just lucky he didn't get put in the hole."

"What was the beating for?" I asked.

Glenn seemed pretty fond of yammering himself, so I figured we might as well learn everything we could.

"Wandered off to some piss-ant town, got his brother killed. Probably the reason the old man took Abe's bride-to-be. Wants to get started on a new brood, providing he can keep her alive long enough. That temper of his has done in an awful lot of wives. Last one didn't make it a week before he stove her head in with a rock."

Glenn laughed again, and shook his head. Charlie and I smiled at him, pretending to see the humor in Hurnen Scault beating a woman to death.

"Why don't you boys go put your horses in the corral. You can go wait by the cabin. Hurnen will take a look at you when he comes out. Can't promise he'll let you stay. And whatever his verdict, you best abide politely. He's not one to tolerate argument."

Glenn went back to his perch on the rock. Charlie and I put our horses up in the makeshift corral. When we were done I noticed Bodaway was still in the saddle.

"I never stay long," Bodaway said. "If I act any different now it's just going to make them suspicious."

"How the Hell are you gonna be any help if you aren't here?" Charlie asked.

"There's a cave," Bodaway said. "It's up on the ledge, above Hurnen's shack. I don't think they know about it. Or if they do they don't care, since there's no way down. I'm going to ride around and come through there."

"What good will you be up there," I asked.

"I got the rifle, and the dynamite," Bodaway said. "I don't need to be close to be effective. Get the girl, get her back here to the horses. I figure it's then you're most likely to need me. If you run into trouble before that just give me a signal."

"Like a whistle, or a bird call?" I asked.

"No need to get fancy," he said. "Just shoot somebody."

TWENTY ONE

Charlie and I made our way through the camp, keeping to the shadows. Even with the coach gun in my arms, the one slung to my back, and the Colt on my hip, I'd never felt so exposed in all my life.

Eli was still over by the fire, so I kept on the lookout for Abe. I could see Charlie was doing the same. Everybody in the camp was armed, and for once my shotguns attracted no attention. As much as it suited our purposes, the ease with which we blended in among this den of murderers and thieves was disturbing to me.

We reached the cabin and sat with our backs against the side wall. Just around the corner was Eli, throwing wood on the fire. It made me nervous to be this close to him, but knowing that Dottie was inside I was reluctant to move. I saw a dead horse laying a little ways off from the fire.

"You reckon that horse is the wedding dinner?" I asked.

"Looks that way," Charlie said. "I'm glad we ain't staying."

"If Eli happens to wander off I say we go inside," I said.

"We don't know how many are in there," Charlie said. "We could get surprised."

"And they won't be expecting us," I said. "So that surprise goes both ways. Plus, I'm betting it's just Hurnen and Dottie."

"You're thinking it's his wedding night and he don't want company," Charlie said.

I was silent. Charlie was right, but I didn't like to think about the matter directly.

"Don't fret over it," Charlie said. "Dottie's made of strong stuff."

Right then Dottie screamed from inside the cabin. I heard a man yell something, and the screaming stopped. No one in the camp reacted to the sounds.

I got to my feet and headed for the door. Charlie grabbed me by the arm.

"If we start shooting now we'll never make it back to the horses," Charlie said.

"Then I'll try not to shoot," I said. "But I'm going in."

Charlie nodded. We walked around to the front of the cabin. Eli looked in our direction, but with our hats pulled low and the bonfire throwing shadows everywhere he didn't recognize us. We opened the door and walked inside.

Eli yelled out from behind us, "You can't go in there. Hey."

Animal skins- coyote, snake, mountain lion and a few that looked an awful lot like people- hung from the ceiling beams like laundry out to dry. So many that you had to push them aside to move through the one room cabin. The heat inside was sweltering.

A man's voice called out from the far end of the cabin. "Jesus on a dead donkey. I said I didn't want to be bothered."

Charlie and I made our way toward the back. I heard the door open behind us and Eli entered, still claiming that we couldn't be in here.

Charlie drew his Colt and looked at me. He put a finger to his lips. I nodded.

We moved a few feet away from each other and waited. Eli's shiny bald head appeared through an opening between two animal hides like some horrifying newborn. Charlie bashed him in the temple with the Colt. Eli grunted, fell to his knees. I reared back and kicked him in the face as hard as I could and the man went down and stayed.

Charlie and I moved forward to the back half of the cabin, which was free from animal skins. I immediately saw Dottie. She was crouched on the ground, her dress torn and dirty. Her left hand was bloody and she clutched it to her chest. Hurnen Scault stood in the center of the space. His white hair hung to his shoulders and was wet with sweat. His beard came down to the middle of his chest and was as white as his hair except for a tobacco stained streak down the center. He wore the patched, filth covered pants of a Confederate soldier. He was shirtless, and his torso was cooked nut-brown from the desert sun. He looked to be near seventy, with dried leathery skin stretched taut over sinew and bone.

"Who in holy fuck are you?" Hurnen said. "I'm performing a holy ceremony. You ain't supposed to be in here."

A strand of rawhide hung around his neck lined with what looked like half-a-dozen pieces of dried jerky. One piece looked fresh and pink. When I looked back at Dottie's bloody hand it came clear to me that Hurnen was wearing a necklace decorated with fingers from his brides.

"Don't shoot him," Charlie said.

His words barely penetrated, but I heard him. I stepped forward and slammed the butt of the shotgun into Hurnen's face. The old man staggered back and I hit him again and he fell.

I felt Charlie put a hand on my shoulder. When I turned to him he held Abe's bowie knife out to me.

"This will be quicker," Charlie said.

I thought about it for a moment. Hurnen was on the ground, blood pouring from his broken nose and teeth. He looked up at me and stared for a long moment.

"You're the one killed Zeke," Hurnen said.

"That's me," I said.

"And I stomped Abe's hat," Charlie said. "On purpose."

"You shouldn't have come here," Hurnen said. "We are protected by God here. You will both be-"

I brought the butt of the shotgun down on the back of his head and he collapsed.

Dottie was still crouched on the floor. She looked from me to Charlie, as if she didn't quite recognize us. Or maybe she just doubted her eyes.

"Owen?" Dottie asked.

"It's me, Dottie," I said.

Dottie got slowly to her feet. She leaned heavily against the wall.

"It's you?" Dottie asked. "It's you? Oh, goddamn. It's really you."

"It really is," I said.

Dottie burst into tears. She came forward and buried her face in my chest. I wrapped my arms around her.

"I kept telling them you'd come," Dottie said. "I told 'em, and I told 'em. Said you were gonna kill every damn one of 'em. They just laughed and I wasn't so sure I believed it myself but here you are just like I said."

Dottie pulled away from me and wiped at her face. She tore a strip from her dress and wrapped her hand as best she could. I helped her, and when it was done she went over and kicked Hurnen four or five times in the ribs. Then she spit on him.

"Bastard took my finger," Dottie said. "Give me that knife, Charlie. I'll cut his pecker off and hang it around his neck."

"I don't doubt he deserves it," Charlie said. "But I think he might scream a little, and we want to avoid the noise if we can. It's time we left anyway. If you're ready."

"I'm ready," Dottie said. "But ain't we gonna kill some of these bastards?"

"Eventually," Charlie said. "But let's see how long we can hold out."

TWENTY TWO

We found some rope in the cabin and used it to tie the hands and feet of Eli and Hurnen. The rope was old and rotten, but it was the best we could do.

"We should just slit their damn throats," Charlie said.

"And cut off their peckers," Dottie said.

"They're no threat at the moment," I said. "We can't just go slitting throats on a whim."

"If they'd done to you what they done to me you wouldn't think it was such a whim," Dottie said.

"Let's just go," I said.

"You remember what I said about your gun mind?" Charlie asked. "Well, this ain't it."

"Do you two really want to stand here arguing about it," I said.

We put my hat on Dottie, and Charlie gave her his jacket. We took Eli's pants for her to wear, which required untying his feet and retying them. It also gave Dottie a chance to put in another vote for pecker chopping, which I vetoed. Once we had Dottie's half-assed disguise in place we made our way through the camp toward the horses.

I looked up at the cliff wall above the cabin, but I

couldn't spot Bodaway. It was dark though, and I figured he would be keeping low. Still, not knowing for sure if he was there made me tense.

We reached the corral, and I stayed with Dottie while Charlie went in and led our horses out. We got Dottie in the saddle, and I was just beginning to breathe easier when everything turned to shit.

A man moved in close and grabbed my arm. I saw the smashed up top hat sitting crookedly on his head and realized it was Abe.

"Where the hell you going?" Abe asked.

He was drunk, and Glen had drastically understated the beating Abe had received. His front teeth were gone, his broken nose was swollen and lay almost sideways on his face. Worst of all was a fist-size knot sprouting from his hairline. If not for the hat I'm not sure I would have recognized the man.

"Cebrelation's about to start," Abe said. "Y'can't go yet."

I began to wonder if Abe was drunk after all. I didn't smell any whiskey on his breath. And looking at that lump on his noggin, I had to wonder if maybe his brains hadn't been scrambled. I saw that he had placed a short stick in the sheath where his Bowie knife once resided. This went a long way toward making me doubt his faculties.

Abe squinted at me, leaning in close. It was painful to watch him try and think.

"Do I know you?" Abe asked.

"You don't know him," Charlie said.

Abe turned to Charlie.

"Do I know you?" Abe asked.

"You don't know either of us," Charlie said.

Abe looked up at Dottie seated on my horse.

"I got to know somesbody," Abe said. "I know every-body here. How about you?"

Dottie shook her head.

Abe stared at her for a long moment. I thumbed back the hammers on my shotgun and looked up one last time, hoping to spot Bodaway.

"Nah, guess I don't know you," Abe said.

Charlie mounted up. He motioned for me to do the same. I was about to climb up behind Dottie when the yelling started. I looked and saw Eli and Hurnen standing by the open door of the cabin. Goddamn rotten rope.

Eli was bare-assed since Dottie had his pants, and he looked a little dazed. Hurnen, despite the beating I'd given him, seemed as vital as ever. He was yelling at everyone in the camp.

"Stop those sonbitches," Hurnen said. "They struck me, and they have stolen my woman."

I saw heads all around the camp turn in our direction. They all seemed confused at the moment, but that wouldn't last long.

"We got to go, hoss," Charlie said.

I was about to respond, when there was a sudden, tearing pain in my shoulder. Abe's stick was sharpened to a point and he'd stabbed me with it. He still had a grip on the end and was working it like a pump handle. I pulled away and he lost his hold on the stick.

I was angry and hurting, and without thinking I brought the ten gauge up, pressed it against his adam's apple, and fired both barrels. Abe's head went spinning off into the dark and the blast sounded like thunder in the canyon. I figured that was plenty of signal for Bodaway.

Glenn stood up on his lookout perch and brought his shotgun to his shoulder. Charlie drew and shot him in the chest. Glenn sat back down and slumped over like he was taking a nap.

I saw Eli charging across the camp. The other men were moving about now and getting in his way, tripping him up. Hurnen was running after him, but he moved with more caution.

There was a gunshot, and my left leg gave out beneath me. I fell and landed on the stick that was still buried in my arm, driving it deeper.

"I want'em alive," Hurnen said. "Anybody kills one of them goes in the hole."

I wrenched the stick out of my arm. Blood poured out so heavy it made me sick to see it. I worked my leg around under me and pulled myself up using the planks of the make-shift corral.

"Go," I said to Charlie.

"Don't you dare, Charlie," Dottie said.

Charlie gave me a curt nod and kicked his horse

into motion. Before Dottie could say another word I slapped her horse on the rump. It took off after Charlie and all she could do was hang on. A couple of grizzled looking fellas tried to pull Charlie from his horse and both got shot in the head for their trouble. Then Charlie and Dottie rode into the narrow pass and out of sight.

I figured I could buy them as much time as possible by keeping these other bastards from their horses. With my injured arm I didn't think I could reload or get the other ten guage out of the sling in before they were on me. I drew my Colt and shot the two nearest men. Hurnen may have wanted me alive, but I wasn't working with the same constraints.

Where the hell was Bodaway? I kept expecting to hear his rifle. Or better still, some of that goddamn dynamite. But there was no sign of him.

Eli was close now. He put his head down and charged me like a bull.

I fired twice and both times all I hit was dirt on either side of him. I wished I had Charlie's aim. I steadied my arm, and was about to put one in the top of his bald head when a rock struck me right between the eyes. My vision blurred, and I felt a moment of embarrassment at being taken down by a rock in the middle of a gunfight. Then Eli slammed into me and drove us both through the corral gate. I landed on my back and Eli came down on top of me, crushing all the air from my lungs. I struggled to draw a breath but there didn't seem to be any air left in that canyon. All I could do was gasp like a fresh caught fish. The spooked horses bolted past us and scattered. I saw Eli's big fist come sailing down at my face, and then I saw nothing at all.

TWENTY THREE

I regained consciousness as I was being carried inside Hurnen's cabin. Men pressed in close, preventing me from moving. Their wild faces loomed over me. For just a moment, when I first woke up, I mistook them for some kind of monsters. As I gradually came to my senses, I understood that I wasn't far wrong.

Their eyes were dead, their faces twisted with glee at the thought of whatever torture awaited me. Along with everything else these men had given up in their flight from the law, living in this hell with Hurnen Scault had stripped them of anything that separated them from animals. They carried me to the back of the cabin where I'd found Dottie and dropped me on the floor. My shoulder throbbed from the stab wound, my leg was numb from being shot, and the way my head hurt I figured the punch I remembered wasn't the only one Eli had delivered.

Hurnen looked down at me. His beard was streaked with blood and his lips were split. I was pleased to see I'd knocked a fair number of teeth from his head.

"I hope to shit I look better than you," I said.

Hurnen kicked me in my injured shoulder and I saw stars.

"You have angered the lord by coming here," Hurnen said. "And now you're gonna be punished."

"I done heard all about this from your boy Abe," I said. "I blew his head plum off his shoulders. Think God's gonna be in a snit about that too?"

That got me another kick in the shoulder. I thought for a second I was going to pass out.

"You are a blaspheming sonbitch," Hurnen said. "I bet that changes after some time in the hole. If you're like most men, you'll be begging God to save you."

"I'm begging him right now," I said. "To save me from having to listen to you."

Hurnen knelt down beside me and leaned in so close I could smell his rotten breath.

"You boys were clever," Hurnen said. "You brought your evil into my sanctuary. In all the Hell you raised your friend even managed to slip away with my woman. But he left you behind to pay the price. That's how it is with evil. No honor, no loyalty. Now is the time to repent, sinner. Tell me where they went, and maybe God's wrath don't have to be so harsh."

"I'll die first," I said.

"You won't," Hurnen said. "But you'll wish you had." Hurnen stood up. He motioned to the men standing nearby.

"Put the sonbitch in the hole," Hurnen said.

A dozen strong hands gripped me, pinned my arms to my sides, lifted me up. I tried to move, to fight them off, but I was weak from blood loss and dizzy from the beating I had taken. My fight didn't amount to much more than saying nasty things about their mothers.

The way the cabin was built up against the side of the canyon, the back wall was bare rock. In the far corner, hidden in the shadows, was a hole in the rock just big enough for a man. And that's where they put me.

TWENTY FOUR

Small spaces have always been a discomfort for me. When I was a shotgun messenger for Wells Fargo I would sit up top next to the driver and imagine being stuck in that tiny coach for all those miles. The thought of it always set my heart to pounding. Compared to the hole, that coach was big as a barn.

The hole sloped slightly downward, and it was just a little over shoulder width. The ceiling was low enough that it touched the tip of my nose. Those boys shoveled me in like bread into an oven.

My arms were pinned to my sides. I couldn't bend my legs. It was completely black and silent. I thought I felt something crawl into my hair.

Even in the dark, even with my eyes closed tight, I could feel the ceiling pressing down on me. It felt like it was crushing my chest, making it hard to draw a full breath. I wanted to scream, but I couldn't seem to get enough air in my lungs.

Hurnen was right. I wished they'd just shot me dead. Anything was better than this.

Panic was building in me, and I felt I was losing myself in my fear. I had to calm my thoughts. It was knowing I was trapped, buried alive, that was driving me mad. I kept going back to the notion that being dead would be preferable, because then there would be no thoughts, no fear, no panic.

So I died in the hole.

At least that's what I told myself. I stopped thinking that I was trapped, and started thinking that I was dead. It was an easy lie to believe there in the dark, in the silence. The hole wasn't a prison, but a grave. There was nothing outside of it, not for me. Not for a dead man.

For a moment I wondered where Dottie and Charlie were. Asked myself why Bodaway hadn't come to our aid. But then I forced those thoughts away. I couldn't allow myself to consider events outside my grave, or the panic would come back.

So I lay dead, in the darkness. No thoughts. No fears. For me, the dead man, there could be only nothingness.

The question of how long I'd been in the hole flitted through my mind. I ignored it. What is time to a dead man? Eventually those stray thoughts stopped troubling me as much, and I was able to still my mind. Finally, when my mind was a perfect blank, images replaced my thoughts. I saw my coach guns, and my Colt. They hung there in my mind, separate from me or any use I might put them too. Just existing. They were disassembled and then reassembled. Cleaned and loaded. A process to repeat, again and again and again. That's how I spent eternity, thinking of nothing but the guns.

TWENTY FIVE

I was pulled from my grave by the boots.

My head banged painfully against the lip of the hole as I fell to the ground. A shaggy haired man with a beard crouched down beside me and slapped at my face. As my eyes adjusted to the light I saw Eli standing a few feet away, grinning at me. He'd found some pants somewhere, but they were too short, and so tight he couldn't fasten them.

"Did you enjoy your time in there?" Eli asked.

I didn't answer. My mind still hadn't adjusted to the fact that I was alive.

"Moses here was impressed you didn't scream," Eli said. "Most men scream."

"Eli screamed," Moses said. "Didn't you, Eli?"

"Not ashamed to say I did," Eli said. "It's dark as murder in there. I never cottoned to the dark."

Moses nudged my shoulder.

"We gonna have some fun with you now," Moses said. "Soon as Pa gets in here with his skinning knife."

I sat up slowly, bent my knees, gradually bringing some life back to my limbs.

"You'll scream for sure then," Eli said.

Moses looked back at Eli and they both laughed.

While I'd been in the hole the thought of my guns had helped calm me. They were far away and seemed to exist only as ideas. But the one gun I hadn't allowed myself to think about was the Marston derringer stowed in my boot. Thinking about it would have given me hope that I could somehow reach it, somehow get out of my situation, and the inability to do so would have driven me out of my mind. Freed from the hole, I remembered it.

While Moses and Eli laughed at the prospect of skinning me alive, I pulled the Marston from my boot, pressed the barrel between Moses' ribs, and shot him twice through the heart.

Eli was in the middle of a laugh when he heard the two little pops and saw Moses fall on his side. He stared at the gun in my hand, confused, a half-smile still on his face.

I pointed the gun at him.

"You tricky sonbitch," Eli said. "But you're out of tricks now. You done shot your load."

There are two things I love about the Marston. The first is that it's a three-shoot derringer, rather than your typical two-shooter. And while it's hard to kill a man with such a small caliber gun unless you're right up on him like I had been with Moses, you can definitely discourage the shit out of him. I did that by shooting Eli in the balls.

Eli fell to his knees, grabbing at himself and

caterwauling. It was an awful sound. Dottie would have approved.

The second thing I love about the Marston is that it has a retractable blade that runs alongside the barrel. Little things like that can make all the difference in the outcome of an ugly encounter.

I snapped the blade in place with a flick of my hand and lunged forward. My legs were still a little wobbly and I started to lose my balance, but I let my momentum carry me to Eli. I shoved the blade into his eye and fell onto him, allowing my weight to drive it into his brain. Eli collapsed under me.

I rolled off of Eli and lay still for a few moments, staring up at the ceiling, collecting myself. Beside me, Eli lay staring up at nothing, the derringer sticking out of his head. His legs twitched violently for several seconds. The movement gradually tapered off, then stopped altogether.

After a minute I got carefully to my feet. I saw my coach guns leaning in the corner. Once I was certain I could remain upright I went to them.

The one I'd fired earlier was still empty. Hurnen's men had taken the extra shells from my pockets before shoving me in the hole. The second shotgun was still in the scabbard, and when I cracked the breach I saw it was loaded.

The shotgun felt good in my hands, familiar in a way it hadn't before. I was in my gun mind now, that was for damn sure. With the ten-gauge in hand, I pushed my way through the hanging skins toward the front of the cabin.

Hurnen Scault threw open the door just as I reached it. He stood framed in silhouette. The sun, nearly blinding me, shone through his mane of white hair and his beard. The blade of the skinning knife glinted sharply in the light. I brought the shotgun to my shoulder and fired both barrels.

Hurnen leaped aside as the shotgun bucked and a chunk of the door frame burst apart. I dropped the shotgun and moved quickly outside.

I'd become so accustomed to the dark I had to hold a hand up to shade my eyes. Men were sprawled everywhere, some hanging half out of their lean-tos, others just passed out on the ground. The horse carcass by the fire was carved up and mostly gone. The canyon smelled of burnt meat and spilled whiskey. Apparently the lack of a bride had not stopped the wedding celebration.

The sound of the shotgun had sent a stir through the camp. Men were beginning to rouse from their drunken slumber. It wouldn't be long before they came to their senses and realized I was among them.

Hurnen lay on his stomach a few feet from the door, pulling himself forward with his right arm. My shot had caught him on the left side and most of that arm was gone. I saw my Colt hanging from the pocket of his britches. I pulled it, checked it, and found that it was loaded.

I put my foot on Hurnen's back, right between his

shoulder blades and pressed down. He squirmed like a bug and made some sort of muttering sounds that might have been prayers. I shot him in the back of the head.

All around the camp the members of Hurnen's gang were gathering their wits, pulling themselves from their sleep and crawling out of their tents. I saw several stumble around looking for their guns. Others had guns but were still too drunk to quickly figure out what was going on. Slowly but surely they turned their attention to me.

I fired at the man closest to me and missed. Gun mind or no, I was still an awful shot.

The man crouched beside his lean-to and drew bead on me with a Sharps. Without looking I could feel myself being lined up in the sights of a dozen other guns.

Then the lean-to blew all to pieces, along with the man and his Sharps.

TWENTY SIX

The explosion knocked me down and took me out of the path of several bullets. I scrambled backwards, stealing a quick glance up at the spot where I expected to see Bodaway. Instead I saw Dottie. She looked wild. Her tangled blond hair glowed in the noonday sun and whipped all around her head as she chucked dynamite down among the men. I could see her lips moving, could tell she was screaming at them, but I couldn't hear a word she was saying. I imagined it had something to do with blowing their peckers off.

Two more explosions shook the earth and I dove inside of the cabin. No breeze could reach inside the canyon, so all the dust and dirt that was stirred up hung in the air like fog. Men tried to run for shelter, but there was none to be had. Wherever they came to light they were soon flying through the air. Or at least pieces of them.

A couple of men tried to enter the cabin and got close enough that I actually managed to shoot them with the Colt. I fired at a few more but only managed to give them a scare.

When the explosions stopped at last, I saw four men gather and advance on the cabin. I waited, hoping they would get close before they began shooting so that I could have a chance of taking at least one or two with me.

Charlie walked out of the cloud of dust behind the men. They turned to face him, and he fanned the hammer of his Colt, firing so fast it sounded like one continuous gunshot. None of the men got off a single shot before they fell dead on the ground.

Charlie leathered his gun and walked over to where I sat just inside the cabin. He looked down at me and grinned.

"Damn, hoss," Charlie said. "You look like you been pulled through a knot-hole backwards. You all right?"

"I've been better," I said.

We walked to the back of the cabin and retrieved my other coach gun and scabbard. I left the Marston in Eli's head. I was just too tired to wrestle it free.

Charlie surveyed the room.

"You did a hell of a job on these boys," Charlie said.

"I like to keep busy," I said.

"Let's light a shuck out of here," Charlie said.

"That suits me right down to the ground."

TWENTY SEVEN

Charlie had to half carry me out of the camp. My injured leg had taken about all the standing it was going to take. My shoulder ached like it had been mule kicked.

As we approached the pass that led us out of the canyon I heard a rifle shot. Then several more.

"Reckon that's Bodaway," Charlie said. "Picking off the few that got by us."

"I figured him for gone," I said. "Considering he didn't lend much of a hand."

"Naw," Charlie said. "He just didn't remember his way around that cave as well as he thought. He stepped into a nest of rattlesnakes and got himself all bit up."

"And he's still alive?" I asked.

"Barely," Charlie said. "When Dottie and me made our break we circled around and rode up the hill. We found Bodaway lying out on the rocks, all swolled up like a tick. We did what we could for him, which wasn't much, then we hunkered down to make our stand. Luckily for us none of these boys could track worth a shit. A few of them rode out and followed our old tracks out into the desert, but they gave up and came back an hour later. Then Dottie and me found our way through the cave and kept watch. We had to wait until we knew for sure where you were before we could start chucking dynamite. When I heard that old ten gauge of yours go off inside the cabin we made our move."

Based on what Charlie told me it seemed that my time in the hole had lasted a little over fourteen hours. Not exactly an eternity. In fact, it seemed downright underwhelming. I decided to keep the whole experience to myself.

When we came out of the hidden entrance to the camp I saw three dead men on the hillside. A little ways further down was Bodaway. He was sitting with his back against a boulder, his Yellow Boy propped up on a rock in front of him. When we got closer I could see that he was in a bad way.

Bodaway's head was puffed up like a pumpkin, and his eyes were little slits. His fingers were so swollen he'd had to remove the trigger guard on the Yellow Boy. I could hear him breathing, all wheezy and loud.

"That the last of them?" Bodaway asked. His voice was thick in his throat.

"Believe it is," Charlie said.

"I thought so," Bodaway said. "So we're even then."

"Yep," Charlie said.

"I'm out of bullets," Bodaway said. "Venom's got my eyes messed up. Took quite a few shots to kill those fellas. If I wasn't out of bullets I would have shot you just now."

"Figured as much," Charlie said.

Bodaway closed his eyes and laid his head back. His breathing grew more labored.

"If you want," Charlie said. "I can send you on your way."

Bodaway opened his puffy eyes. "Hell no. I might pull through."

"I suppose anything's possible," Charlie said.

With great effort, Bodaway shifted around and pulled his knife from his boot. He clutched it in both swollen hands.

"I'm gonna rest a bit," Bodaway said. "Then you and I are gonna tangle. Don't shoot me while I'm asleep."

"I won't," Charlie said.

Bodaway closed his eyes and was still except for the rising and falling of his chest. Charlie and I walked on and soon we could no longer hear Bodaway's wheezing. Our horses waited at the bottom of the hill and as we got near, Dottie rode up on Bodaway's paint. She practically jumped off the horse and ran to hug me.

Up on the cliff she had looked like an avenging angel, but up close she looked like something feral. Her face was smeared with dirt, her dress in rags. Her wild blond hair looked like last year's nest, and she smelled of gunpowder. After she finished hugging me Dottie set about tending my wounds. Luckily my leg wasn't broken, just had a bullet hole through my thigh. The shoulder was the worst. Abe had stabbed me deep.

Bodaway had some whiskey in one of his saddle bags and Dottie used it to clean the hell out of both wounds.

It hurt almost as bad as getting shot and stabbed in the first place. Dottie tore off a few more strips from her dress and one of my sleeves, and when she was done I was bandaged up tight.

"Don't you think we ought to leave one of these horses for Bodaway?" Dottie asked once we'd mounted up.

"Bodaway needs a horse, he'll find one," Charlie said. "But I don't reckon he'll be needing one."

"Besides," I said. "If he pulled through we'd just have to kill him."

Charlie and Dottie both looked at me funny.

"Well, we would," I said.

"That's true enough," Charlie said.

We mounted up and rode back the way we came, none of us saying much. I considered all the dead men back in the canyon, and I found that their deaths did not weigh on me. I didn't question the right or wrong of it, and I felt no pangs of guilt. The necessity had been clear, and that was enough to satisfy my conscience.

Despite the aches and pains of my injuries, I felt fine. I felt a certainty about myself that I hadn't known before our trip across the desert, before my time in the hole. I considered our burned down saloon, and knew without a doubt that we wouldn't be rebuilding. Charlie had been right, we weren't cut out to run a business. Our skills lay elsewhere. I understood at last that like it or not, we were gunmen.

Thank you for reading **Gunmen**, the first in the Brittle and Ashe series. If you enjoyed the book please leave a review online. As a bonus, here is the first chapter of **Guns of October**, the next Brittle and Ashe adventure.

GUNS OF OCTOBER
By Timothy Friend
Available March 2021

ONE

Of all the occupations Charlie Brittle and I had tried over the years, it was man-hunting that suited us best.

We'd only been bounty-hunters for a short time, but had proven to be naturals at it. The only problem we had was our differing views on how to interpret the decree 'Wanted: Dead or Alive'. The way I read it, the choice was an offer you made to the fugitive- surrender, or face the gun. To Charlie's way of thinking, if the law really wanted their man alive they would have put that part first.

We solved the matter by alternating our approach. Charlie's approach didn't amount to much more than walking up and shooting a man, often in front of a group of shocked and suddenly skittish onlookers. Times like that, it fell on me to show the paper we had on the dead man, settle everyone's nerves before more shooting broke out. I sometimes suspected that Charlie enjoyed the drama of it all and wouldn't have minded a little more shooting if it came to that.

I'd like to say there was less killing when we did things my way and announced ourselves and our intentions proper like. There wasn't. The men we pursued were mean, vicious, short-sighted sonbitches who just could not foresee things going badly for them. Inevitably they would make their play and we would shoot them dead.

This never bothered Charlie, but I found it so disheartening I was ready to go back to running our saloon, if not for the fact that it had been burned to the ground, and we hadn't made any money at it in the first place. Just about the time I'd given up on the notion of collecting a bounty on someone we hadn't first filled full of holes we met Fat-Boy Barker.

Fat-Boy, along with his partner in murder and thievery Jimmy Thistle, had robbed a stagecoach and killed two passengers in the process before lighting out for East Texas. Charlie and I picked up their trail in Beaumont and followed their path along the Sabine River. I kept getting the nagging feeling that we were being followed, and I told Charlie about it.

Charlie said, "We know Fat-Boy and Jimmy are ahead of us, so what's your worry."

"My worry," I said, "Is whoever's behind us."

"That would be nobody."

I said, "I'm telling you, Charlie, ever since we left Beaumont, whenever I look behind me I get the feeling like somebody just stepped out of sight. Why do you think that is?"

After thinking it over for a minute, Charlie said, "I don't believe there's anybody back there, I think it's just the jitters. But I can see you're convinced. What do you want to do?"

I said, "Nothing I guess. You're probably right."

Charlie said, "Don't agree just to get along. I don't want to hear any 'I told you so' if I'm wrong."

"Oh, you'll for sure be hearing that. If it turns out I picked up on somebody following us before the great Charlie Brittle, you'll be hearing 'I told you so' for the rest of your born days. On my deathbed I'll be saying, 'I told you so'."

Charlie said, "On your deathbed? So you plan on dying before me?"

I said, "Maybe I'm old and dotty and just forgot that you died already. Probably in some embarrassing and dishonorable way that pains me to think about."

Charlie nodded, said, "I can see that."

Eventually Fat-Boy's trail left the main road and followed a less travelled path that led Charlie and me into dense woods. Even with Charlie's belief to the contrary, I still had the sense that somebody was behind us, dogging our every step.

Despite the healthy lead they had on us it seemed as if we were gaining on Fat-Boy and his partner with relative ease. It wasn't long before we were finding tracks that appeared no more than a day old. It was like they didn't care they were being pursued. Wasn't until we caught up with them that it finally made sense to me.

It was early morning when we found our men near the river. After spotting their tracks, Charlie and I decided to tie off our horses and pack mule and creep up on foot, the better to catch them by surprise. We found their camp and the two of us crouched in the brush to look things over. I spotted Jimmy Thistle sleeping soundly by a smoldering campfire, and snoring loud as a rockslide. It looked like a horse was lying on the ground beside him draped in a blanket, but when I saw both their horses tied to a nearby tree I realized I was mistaken.

I said, "That big heap there, covered in the dirty blanket?"

Charlie said, "Fat-Boy."

"Damn. No wonder they were so slow-travelling."

Charlie said, "He's a big boy all right. You still want to do it your way, Owen? We could just shoot'em both right here and be perfectly within the law."

"You can't be serious. Even you wouldn't shoot a couple of fellas in their sleep."

Charlie said, "Nah. First I'd yell something like, 'Wake up boys, it's judgement day.' Then I'd shoot'em."

I shook my head, said, "Sometimes you scare me."

"Your desire to palaver with men who want us dead don't exactly do my heart good."

"Fair point. But these boys are asleep, so this should go better."

"It'll go different," Charlie said. "Not so sure it'll be better."

We stood up then and stepped from the brush into the clearing. Charlie had one of his Colts in hand, the hammer thumbed back. I carried my .10 gauge cradled in my arms. I was a terrible shot, but the shotgun, a keepsake from my days riding for Wells Fargo, compensated for my lack of marksmanship. I had a second one back with my horse. I often carried it in a scabbered on my back, but had learned from experience that it was a hindrance when creeping around in thick woods.

True to his word, as we approached the sleeping men Charlie yelled, "Wake up, boys. Judgement day has arrived."

Neither man stirred. Jimmy's snoring carried on, loud and steady.

I said, "I'm guessing that's not the reaction you expected."

Charlie gave me a sour look. Then he said, "Get up, you sidewinders. The wrath of justice is upon you."

Jimmy smacked his lips, shifted a little there on the hard ground, then his snoring escalated from rockslide to full-on avalanche.

Charlie said, "Lazy sonbitches are spoiling my entrance." Then he fired his gun in the air.

Jimmy bolted upright, his head craning this way and that, his bug-eyes trying to see everywhere at once. Fat-Boy woke just as quickly, but it took a considerable amount of time and effort for him to work himself into a sitting position. When he saw Charlie and me, our guns aimed at him, his big shoulders drooped.

Fat-Boy said, "I never should have come to Texas."

I said, "We aim to take you boys back to Beaumont,

turn you over to the law. The only decision you have to make is how many new holes you want to arrive with."

Jimmy said, "None for me, thanks. I don't expect Fat-Boy here wants any either."

Fat-Boy said, "I can speak for my own damn self."

I said, "Yeah? So what's it going to be."

Fat-Boy craned his neck to look at me. His face was round and jowly, his eyes so deep set they were just black dots. When he spoke it sounded like the words were being throttled by the rolls of fat around his neck.

He sighed, said, "I don't want no new holes either."

Jimmy said, "All you did was tell'em what I already told'em."

Fat-Boy said, "Shut up."

"All I'm saying is, you make a big deal out of me speaking for you and then you go and say the same thing I did."

Fat-Boy said, "And all I'm saying is shut up."

Charlie looked at me, said, "Can I shoot'em now?"

Jimmy put both his hands in the air, said, "We done surrendered. No need to shoot nobody."

I said, "Put your hands down and stand up. Nobody's going to shoot you long as you move slow and easy."

Jimmy lowered his hands and stood up. "Only way I can move. Sleeping on the goddamn ground has me so stiff I can hardly stand up straight."

Charlie said, "I don't care if you stay bent at the waist. Just unfasten that gunbelt and leave it on the ground."

Jimmy unbuckled his belt and let it drop. He kept on complaining. "I'm not cut out for sleeping rough. Goddamn chiggers are eating me alive. Only food we got is beans. And let me tell you, you don't want to travel downwind of Fat-Boy if beans is all you got on the menu. I'm so sick of smelling farts and sleeping in the woods, if I'd known you were looking for us I would have come found you."

Charlie waved his gun at Fat-Boy, said, "You too, big fella."

After working at it some Fat-Boy got to his feet. His big belly hung down and covered his belt buckle and it took a good deal of hoisting for him to undo it. I could tell it was making Charlie nervous watching the man's hand move around so close to his gun. I expected him to say the hell with it and shoot Fat-Boy, but despite his unease Charlie showed restraint.

Fat-Boy stared down at his gunbelt when it hit the ground, said again, "I never should have come to Texas."

Jimmy said, "It's a long ride back to Beaumont. What kind of grub you boys carrying."

I hesitated before saying, "Mostly beans."

Jimmy looked like he was about to cry, said, "Shit. You fellas mind if I check my line?"

He pointed toward the riverbank where a piece of twine hung from a tree branch down into the water. The line was pulled tight, and it moved ever so slightly as I watched it.

Jimmy said, "I strung it last night, hoped we might

catch a fish for breakfast. Maybe a snapping turtle. Hell, even an old boot would be better than more beans."

Jimmy didn't wait for either Charlie or I to give the ok, just walked over to the tree and leaned out to grab the line. The twine was pulled out at an angle, making it difficult to reach from shore. Jimmy grabbed an overhead branch with one hand and reached out with the other far as he could, stretching himself out over the water.

He kept up a steady patter. "Looks like I might have caught something. I'll share it with you boys if you like. I can cook up a catfish will bring tears to your eyes."

There was an old log just under the surface of the water, and I saw Jimmy's foot come down on it as he struggled to get enough reach to grab the twine. The log shifted, and I expected it to roll out from under his foot at any moment and drop Jimmy in the river.

Jimmy was still telling us about his skill at cooking catfish. "My old gramma taught me how to do it up right. The most important thing to remember when you cook a catfish is-"

I never learned the secret to cooking catfish because right then there was an explosion of water and mud and sharp teeth and all at once an alligator clamped its jaws around Jimmy Thistle's head.

Guns of October coming March of 2021